Suddenly, Sam knew he wasn't the only one who had been carrying a torch for the last ten years.

Lulu still had feelings for him, too.

The next thing he knew, she was in his arms. Her face turned up to his, and in that instant, all the pain of the last decade melted away. Their lips fused. A low helpless sound escaped her throat and she pressed herself against him, yielding to him the way she had never surrendered before.

And damn it all, if he wasn't giving his all to her, too. He gathered her even closer, let the sexy kiss deepen, all the while savoring the sweet womanly taste of her, her fiery temperament, her fragrance, her warmth and her tenderness. Whether or not they'd be able to work it all out in the long haul was still questionable, but there'd never been anyone else for him. Never would be...

* * *

TEXAS LEGENDS: THE McCABES
Three Generations and counting

Dear Reader,

No one wants to disappoint others or be disappointed themselves. But it happens. The challenge is dealing with it. Finding a way to be happy—and to make others feel the same—without giving up anything that is fundamentally important or essential to you.

Lulu McCabe is feeling the pressure. The only daughter of Frank and Rachel McCabe, and sister to her five brothers, she is constantly protected and advised. Some of the attention is warranted, she admits. It took her a while to figure out what she wanted to do with her life. She definitely made some Big Mistakes along the way. And she knows that if her family ever learned about the most important one, wow, would they ever be disappointed in her!

Sam Kirkland is her direct opposite. He doesn't give a hoot what others say or think as long as he knows in his gut, and his heart, that he is doing the right thing. Of course, he's made some Big Mistakes, too. The most devastating with his current nemesis, and former girlfriend, Lulu McCabe. He has no more use for her than she has for him, until three orphaned triplets enter their lives. The duty is Sam's. Lulu's only Backup Guardian should Sam fail, and Sam has absolutely no intention of crashing and burning the way he and Lulu once did.

Of course, we all know what happens when we're busy making other plans. Life. And in this life, Lulu and Sam and those three little boys are meant to be together. The only question is, will Sam and Lulu be able to rekindle their love? Here's hoping!

Happy reading!

Cathy Gillen Thacker

Their Inherited Triplets

Cathy Gillen Thacker

HARLEQUIN® SPECIAL EDITION

Recycling programs
for this product may
not exist in your area.

ISBN-13: 978-1-335-57402-2

Their Inherited Triplets

Copyright © 2019 by Cathy Gillen Thacker

This edition published by arrangement with Harlequin Books S.A.

For questions and comments about the quality of this book,
please contact us at CustomerService@Harlequin.com.

Printed in U.S.A.

Cathy Gillen Thacker is married and a mother of three. She and her husband spent eighteen years in Texas and now reside in North Carolina. Her mysteries, romantic comedies and heartwarming family stories have made numerous appearances on bestseller lists, but her best reward, she says, is knowing one of her books made someone's day a little brighter. A popular Harlequin author for many years, she loves telling passionate stories with happy endings and thinks nothing beats a good romance and a hot cup of tea! You can visit Cathy's website, cathygillenthacker.com, for more information on her upcoming and previously published books, recipes, and a list of her favorite things.

Books by Cathy Gillen Thacker

Harlequin Special Edition

Texas Legends: The McCabes

The Texas Cowboy's Quadruplets
His Baby Bargain

Harlequin Western Romance

Texas Legacies: The Lockharts

A Texas Soldier's Family
A Texas Cowboy's Christmas
The Texas Valentine Twins
Wanted: Texas Daddy
A Texas Soldier's Christmas

Visit the Author Profile page
at Harlequin.com for more titles.

Chapter One

"What are *you* doing here?" Lulu McCabe rose to her feet and gaped at the big, strapping cowboy with the wheat-blond hair and the mesmerizing gold-flecked eyes. Even with a good ten feet and a huge table between them, just the sight of him made her catch her breath.

Sam Kirkland strolled into the conference room at their Laramie, Texas, lawyers' office in his usual commanding way. He offered her a sexy half smile that warmed her from the inside out. "I could ask the same of you, darlin'."

With a scowl, Lulu watched as he came around the table to stand beside her.

Clad in jeans, a tan shirt and boots, his Resistol held politely against the center of his broad chest, he was the epitome of the highly successful, self-made rancher. The way he carried himself only added to his inherent masculine appeal.

Ignoring the shiver of awareness pooling inside her, Lulu looked him square in the eye. "So, you don't know what this is about, either?" she guessed finally.

"Nope." He gave her a leisurely once-over, then narrowed his eyes at her, as always appearing to blame her for every calamity that came their way. "I figured you engineered it."

Anger surged through her, nearly as strong as the attraction she'd worked very hard to deny.

Lulu drew a breath and inhaled the brisk, masculine fragrance of his cologne and the soapy-fresh scent of his hair and skin. Determined to show him just how completely she had gotten over him, she stepped closer, intentionally invading his space. "Why would I want to do that?"

He held her eyes deliberately. Gave her that slow smile, the one that always turned her legs to jelly. "Honestly, darlin'," he taunted in a low tone, "I don't know why you want to do *lots* of things."

Really? He was going to go back to their last argument, claiming she was not making any sense? Again? Slapping both her hands on her hips, she fumed, "Listen, cowboy, you know exactly why I want to join the Laramie County Cattleman's Association!"

His gaze drifted over her before she could make her proposal again. "And you know exactly why, as organization president, I'm not about to let you."

She had a good idea. And it had a lot to do with what had secretly happened between them a little over a decade ago. With exaggerated sweetness, she guessed, "Because you're not just a horse's behind, but a stubborn, sexist mule, too?"

Finally, his temper flared, as surely as her own. He blew out a frustrated breath, then lowered his face to hers. "It's not enough to just own a ranch in Laramie County, Lulu," he reiterated.

Both hands knotted at her sides, she glared up at him, aware her heart was pounding, and lower still, there was a building heat. "Well, it should be!" she argued right back.

"You have to raise cattle. Not honeybees."

"Okay, you two, calm down." Family law attorney Liz Cartwright Anderson breezed into the conference room, her husband and law partner right behind her.

"Or someone might think something besides a show of heat is going on with you," Travis Anderson quipped.

"The only thing we share is an immense dislike of each other," Lulu grumbled. *Well, that, and an unwillingness to forgive.* Because if they had been able to do that… things might be different now. But they hadn't… So…

Liz sent a questioning look at Sam. He lifted an amiable hand. "What she says," he quipped.

An awkward silence fell.

"We could meet with you separately," Travis offered finally. "Since Sam is my client, and Lulu is Liz's."

Lulu shook her head. They wouldn't have been called in together unless the matter involved them both. "Let's just get it over with," she groused.

"Okay, then." Liz smiled. "Travis and I called you both here together because we have some very important things to discuss," she began, as a somber-looking man with buzz-cut silver hair walked in to join them. He was dressed in a suit and tie, carrying a briefcase and appeared to be in his late fifties.

Travis made the formal introductions. "This is Hiram Higgins. He's an estate attorney from Houston. He's enlisted our help in making what we hope will be a smooth transition."

"*Transition?* For what?" Lulu blurted, glancing over at Sam. For once, the big, sexy cowboy looked as clueless as she was. Unsure whether to take comfort in that or not, she opened her mouth to speak again.

Liz lifted a hand. "It will all become clear in a moment. Why don't we all sit down?" she suggested kindly.

Everyone took the chair closest to them, which put Sam and Lulu on one side of the table and Liz and Travis opposite them.

Hiram took a chair at the head of the table and opened up his briefcase. "There's no easy way to say this," he said, "so I am going to plunge right in. I'm handling the estate of Peter and Theresa Thompson. They were killed in an auto accident in Houston two months ago."

Lulu sucked in a breath. She hadn't seen her sophomore year roommate, Theresa, and her husband, Peter—one of Sam's old college friends—since the two had eloped years before, but shock and sorrow tumbled through her. Sam seemed equally taken aback by the tragic loss. He reached over and put his hand on top of hers.

Normally, Lulu would have resisted his touch. But right now, she found she needed the warm, strong feel of his fingers draped over hers.

She actually needed more than that.

Given the grief roiling around inside her, a hug wouldn't have been out of bounds...

Had the person beside her been anyone but the man who had stomped her heart all to pieces, of course.

Unobtrusively, Lulu withdrew her hand from his.

Hiram continued, "Peter and Theresa left three sons, two-year-old triplets."

Lulu struggled to take this all in. Regretting the fact they'd all lost touch with each other, she asked hoarsely, "Where are the children now?"

"In Houston."

"With family?" Sam ascertained.

Hiram grunted in the affirmative. "And friends. Temporarily. We're keeping them together, of course. Which is where the two of you come in." He paused to give both Lulu and Sam a long, steady look.

"Peter and Theresa came to see me shortly after their children were born. They wanted to make out wills, but sadly, were never able to agree on who should take care of their children in the event something happened to them. So, they did what a lot of people do when it comes to thorny guardianship issues. They agreed to discuss it some more…and put off finalizing anything with my office."

He cleared his throat. "In the meantime, they went on one of those do-it-yourself legal websites and made out practice wills. They never had those notarized, so they aren't official and may or may not hold up in probate court. But thanks to the copies they left behind, we do have their wishes on record, which is what we are using to guide us now."

"And those wishes are…?" Sam prodded.

After a long silence, Hiram finally said, "Sam, you were Peter's third choice for legal guardian. And Lulu, you were Theresa's fourth choice."

Third! And fourth! "Who was first?" Lulu asked, curious.

Hiram looked down at his notes. "Theresa chose the great-aunt who raised her. Mabel had the boys for about two weeks, before she fell and broke her hip."

Sam and Lulu exchanged concerned looks.

"From there, they went to Peter's first choice—his best friend, Bob, who is also a father of three, all under age five."

Sam nodded, listening.

"The kids all got along great, even if it was something of a madhouse. Unfortunately, Bob's wife is pregnant and had to go on bed rest for the duration of her pregnancy."

Lulu sighed in dismay.

"So, the triplets then went to Theresa's second choice—a cousin of hers who is a flight attendant." Hiram frowned. "Olivia had them for a week and a half before deciding there was no way she was cut out for this."

He looked up. Adding in concern, "From there, they went to Peter's second cousin. Aaron's engaged and wants a lot of kids, but his fiancée is not on board with the idea of a ready-made family. So that trial run also didn't work out."

"And now…?" Lulu asked, her heart going out to the children for all they had been through.

"They are with Theresa's business colleague and her husband. Unfortunately, although they adore the boys and vice versa, they both travel a lot for work, so permanent guardianship is not a viable option there, either. Which brings us to Sam, the last person on Peter's list."

"Or…actually, me," Lulu interjected with her usual gung ho enthusiasm for all things family. She was more than ready to take on the challenge. "If you just want to cut to the chase."

Sam didn't know why he was surprised Lulu was jumping headlong into a situation neither of them was cut out for. She'd always been romantic and impulsive. Never more so, it seemed, than when she was around him.

The trouble was, he felt passionate and impractical around her, too.

Part of it was her looks. She really was drop-dead gorgeous, with that thick mane of sun-kissed, honey-brown hair, those long-lashed turquoise blue eyes, elegant cheekbones and cute, determined chin. And she had impeccable fashion sense, too. Her five-foot-eight-inch frame was currently decked out in a short-sleeved black polo, bearing the Honeybee Ranch logo above one luscious breast, a snug-fitting dark denim skirt that made the most of her trim hips and long, lissome legs, and a pair of Roper boots that were as sturdy as they were feminine. She had movie-star sunglasses on top of her head, a leather-banded watch on her left wrist and four handmade bracelets, probably made by her four nieces, pushed high on the other.

But it was the skeptical twist of her soft, kissable lips as she leaned toward him and shot him a disdainful look that captivated him the most.

"Let's be real here," she said, inundating him with the scent of her signature fragrance, an alluring combination of flowers and citrus, along with a heady dose of that saucy attitude he recalled so well. "There's no way you're going to take on two-year-old triplets for more than a week or so without changing your mind, too, the way everyone else who's had them already has."

The fact she had such a low opinion of him stung. Unable to keep the growl out of his voice, he challenged, "What makes you think that?"

"Because." Lulu shrugged, her eyes taking on a turbulent sheen. "You're a man...and you're busy running a big cattle ranch...and you're single..."

All of which, last time he'd heard, were facts in his favor. "And you're a woman. And you're busy running a honeybee ranch and now a food truck, too. And you're single."

Lulu's mouth dropped into an O of surprise. She squared her shoulders and tried again. "The point is, *cowboy*—" she angled her thumb at her chest "—I'm cut out for this."

He let his glance sift over her from head to toe before returning, with even more deliberation, to her eyes. "Really?" he countered softly. As always, when they were together, the world narrowed to just the two of them. "'Cause I am, too."

Indignant color flooded her cheeks. "Sam, come on, be reasonable!" She gave him a look he was hard-pressed to reject. "I've wanted a family forever."

He cocked his head to one side, once again forcing himself to do what was best, instead of letting his emotions get the better of him. "Mmm-hmm. Well, so do I, darlin'."

She stared at him. He stared back. Years of pent-up feelings entered the mix and combined with the ever-encompassing grief and sense of loss. Both feelings she seemed to be struggling with, too. Then, breaking the silent standoff, she pushed her chair back from the table and pivoted to face him. As always, when overwrought, she let her temper take charge. "You're just volunteering to do this in order to be difficult."

Actually, he was trying to honor their late friends' wishes, and keep them all from being hurt any more than they already had been. "You couldn't be more wrong, Lulu."

"Is that right? Then please, enlighten me."

With a grave look, hoping to get through to her once and for all, he said, "I'm taking this on because Peter was once a very good friend of mine, and he trusted me to care for his sons, if the worst ever happened. Since it has…" Sam's voice caught. Pushing his sorrow aside, he went on huskily, "I will."

Hiram interjected, "Y'all understand. The request isn't binding. You both are free to say no."

Lulu turned back to the children's lawyer. "And if we *were* to do so?" she asked in concern.

Hiram said, "Then we'd notify social services in Houston and have the agency start looking for suitable adoptive parents."

Not surprisingly, Sam noted, Lulu looked as upset by the thought of leaving the kids at the mercy of the system as he was. Once again, without warning, the two of them were on the exact same page.

"And in the meantime?" he asked gruffly.

Hiram explained, "They'll be put in foster care."

"Together?" Lulu queried.

Hiram's face took on a pained expression. "I would hope so. But honestly, there's no guarantee a placement like that could be found, at least right away."

Lulu sighed, appearing heartbroken. "Which would likely devastate the children."

Hiram nodded.

She swung back toward Sam, and concluded sadly, "So, it's either going to be you, or it's going to be me, taking these three kids on and raising them." She gave him a long, assessing look. "And you have to know, deep down, which one of us is better suited for parenting toddlers."

He did.

Although he doubted they agreed.

"Which is why, given the options that are left," Sam said, pushing aside his own welling grief, and ignoring the pleading in her soft turquoise blue eyes, "I think I'm the right one to assume responsibility."

"Okay, then," Hiram declared, looking happy everything had been resolved so very quickly. He reached into the folder in front of him and brought out a file of paperwork. "I'll make arrangements to have the boys brought to Laramie County as soon as possible. All you'll need to do is sign here—"

"Whoa! Wait! *That's it?*" Lulu sputtered. "You're not even going to ask me if I'm interested in being the triplets' legal guardian?"

Hiram paused, papers still in hand. "Are you?"

"Yes! Very!" Hands clasped tightly, she leaned toward the estate lawyer urgently. "I would love to do this for Peter and Theresa's boys!"

"Until it starts to get hard and reality sinks in," Sam muttered, thinking of their torrid past, and knowing there was no way he would visit such a reversal of fortune on those boys. "Then we both know where you will be, don't we, darlin'?" he returned bitterly. "Out the door. Without so much as a look back."

Lulu glared at him. "I'm not a quitter, Sam," she told him fiercely.

Wasn't she? It seemed like that was exactly what she had done ten years ago, albeit in a roundabout way. He regarded her skeptically. "But you are still very emotional. And impetuous." Two character traits that were intensified by their mutual sense of loss.

Lulu winced. "And you're overbearing and hopelessly set in your ways, so—"

Travis let out a referee-style whistle, signaling everyone needed to stop before anyone else said anything regrettable, no matter how upset they were. He turned to his wife, giving her the floor.

"Obviously," Liz interjected gently but firmly, "this has been a tremendous shock, and we're all feeling a little emotional and overwrought right now."

"Which is why, on second thought," Hiram concurred, putting the papers back in his briefcase before leveling a look at Sam, "I'm going to ask you to take a little more time to think about this." After a beat, Hiram contin-ued, "If, after due consideration, you still feel inclined to accept temporary guardianship, you can call me and let me know, and I'll arrange to have the boys and their belongings driven here. The guardianship papers can be signed when you take custody of them."

"What about me?" Lulu said, clearly hurt and disap-pointed.

Hiram stood. "As I said, you're next in line if things don't go well with Sam and the boys. But for right now," the lawyer said firmly, "he is the one being tapped to take care of the triplets."

The meeting broke up.

Sam and Lulu walked outside.

As they reached their respective vehicles, she studied him with wary reserve. "How are you going to do this?"

It irked him to realize she did not think he could. He squinted down at her. "One step at a time."

"I'm serious, Sam!"

He shrugged. "Obviously," he drawled, "I'll need help."

Lulu opened her mouth to respond just as her cell phone went off. She plucked it out of her purse and stared disbelievingly at the text message.

Concerned, Sam stepped closer. "What is it?" he asked.

Her brow furrowed. In a dumbfounded tone, she admit-ted, "The sheriff's department has been called to my ranch!"

Chapter Two

An hour and a half later, Lulu stood at the entrance of the apiary on her ranch, staring at the empty field. Bare spots where the boxes and pallets had been. A few wooden lids scattered here and there. The occasional honeybee buzzing around, wondering where in the world the hives had gone.

"Are you okay?" Sam asked, standing next to her, looking more solid and imperturbable than ever.

Was she?

Resisting the urge to throw herself into his arms and ask for the comfort only he could give, Lulu turned away from his quiet regard. Her heart aching, she watched the patrol car leave her ranch. The only time she had ever felt this devastated was when Sam had walked away from her years ago in Tennessee. But she had survived heartbreak then, she told herself steadfastly. And she would survive it now.

"Lulu?" he prompted again.

She pivoted back toward him and lifted her chin, hating that he had to see her at her most vulnerable. "Of course I'm all right," she muttered. Although the devastation might have been easier to bear had he not gallantly insisted on accompanying her to the scene of the crime. And then, once amid the devastation, done his best to assist her and the sheriff's deputy who'd been sent to investigate. Because that had made her want to lean on him, the way she once had. And she knew she could never do that again.

Oblivious to the morose direction of her thoughts, Sam put a staying hand on her shoulder. Moved so she had no choice but to look into his face. Solemnly, he reminded her, "It's been a hell of a day, darlin'. First, we found out about the death of our close friends. Learned their boys had been orphaned. And found out we had both been tapped as potential guardians. Now, you just had all three hundred of your bee boxes, as well as your entire stockpile of honey, stolen."

Which left her with exactly nothing, she realized miserably. Seven years of hard work, building up her hives, gone. The only thing she had left of her business, aside from her small 150-acre ranch property, was her Honeybee Ranch food truck, and without her signature honey, the food she served out of that wasn't going to be the same, either.

His gaze drifting over her with unexpected gentleness, Sam told her, "I called the other officers of the Laramie County Cattleman's Association while you were talking to the deputy, and put out the word. Everyone's offered to do whatever they can to help."

Lulu was grateful for the assistance. Even if she wasn't entirely sure it would do much good now, after the theft. With a grimace, she stepped back. Despite her efforts to the contrary, she was unable to control the emotions riding roughshod inside her.

Bitter tears misting her eyes, she blurted out, "If only you had made that offer prior to today, cowboy, I might not be in such a mess."

Recognition lit his gold-flecked eyes. "Wait…" He touched her arm and surveyed her. "Is *that* why you were so determined to join the Laramie County Cattleman's Association? Because you were *afraid* something like this could happen?"

Shoulders stiff, she shrank from his touch. "What did you think?" she scoffed. "That it was for your charming company?"

Stepping closer, he cupped her shoulders between his large palms, preventing her escape. "Why didn't you just tell me this?"

As if it had been that easy, given his resistance to cutting her even the slightest bit of slack, after what had happened between them.

His tranquil manner grating on her nerves as much as his chivalrous attitude, Lulu broke free from his hold and spun away. Her pulse skittering, she headed toward the barn. "I would have, had I felt you would be the least bit sympathetic or helpful." She tossed the words over her shoulder, then turned her glance forward again. "But you weren't…so…" An ache rose in her throat.

Sam caught up with her, matching her stride for indignant stride. "Come on, Lulu," he said. "It's not as if you've ever been afraid to fight any battle with me."

Lulu stopped dead in her tracks. He was right. She wasn't afraid to go toe-to-toe with him. Never had been. With effort, she forced herself to be honest. Wearily, she said, "In the end, I didn't come to you with my fears because even though I knew it was happening in other parts of the state, big-time, I wasn't really sure something like this could ever happen here in Laramie County." She sighed. "Or maybe I just didn't want to believe that it would. Especially since I'm the only beekeeper who runs—or did run, anyway—a big commercial operation."

"And the other beekeepers?" Sam didn't take his eyes off her.

Lulu felt the heat of his gaze like a caress. "Are simply hobbyists, with one or two hives, so it really wouldn't be worthwhile for anyone to go in and try to locate and then steal their boxes."

She went into the barn, came out with a wooden pallet and carried it over to the apiary. She wanted any remaining bees in the area to have a place to go.

Sam kept pace with her, inundating her with his brisk, masculine scent. He watched her set down the pallet in the middle of the barren field. "Why would they want to do that, anyway? I mean, given the risk of getting caught?"

She returned to the barn for a brand-new wooden bee box bearing the Honeybee Ranch brand and a metal water pan. Already thinking about getting a new queen for the hive. "Because adding hives to orchards can increase the yield up to four hundred percent." At his look of amazement, she added, "I've had offers to rent out my bees to almond orchards in California, watermelon fields in south Texas and cranberry bogs in Wisconsin."

His large frame blocking out the late-afternoon June sunshine, Sam stood back and gave her room to work. "And you said no?"

Acutely aware of his fiercely masculine presence, she carried both items over to the pallet inside the apiary. Set the lidded box down, filled a water pan from the outdoor faucet and left it nearby. "Every time."

His brow furrowed. She could see he didn't understand.

Sighing, she explained, "I could earn money that way, but it'd be hard on my bees, and it would bring with it risk of mites and disease and infection to the hives. Which would not be worth it in my opinion, since I already have a very good market for my honey. Or had."

Briefly, guilt and remorse etched the handsome features of his face. "I'm so sorry, darlin'."

Again. Too little, too late.

Arms folded, she moved even farther away.

Gruffly, he promised, "We'll find your bees, Lulu."

She dug in her heels. Now was not the time for idle comfort, just as earlier had not been the time for idle promises. "And if we don't?" The tears she'd been holding back flooded her eyes. "Then what?" She blotted the moisture with her fingertips. "I'm going to have to start my honey business *all over*, Sam."

He shook his head, stubbornly nixing even the possibility of that outcome. "Someone had to have seen something unusual, even if they didn't put it together at the time. With the sheriff's department and the cattleman's association both working on finding answers ASAP, we should know something soon."

Would they? Lulu wished she could be as certain of that as Sam. Heck, she wished she had even a tenth of his confidence.

"In the meantime," he continued in an agreeable tone that warmed her through and through, "I'd like to help you in whatever way I can."

Lulu studied him. "Do you mean that?" she asked thickly, turning her attention to the other big challenge currently facing her. The one with even more potential to break her heart. "Because if you do," she said slowly,

"I've got a proposition for you." She paused, bracing for battle. "I'd like to be the children's nanny."

Sam had known that Lulu would not accept him as the triplets' guardian when she was next on the list. And hence she would continue to fight the decision, in one way or another.

But he hadn't expected her to offer this.

"*You*...want to be the triplets' nanny?" he repeated in disbelief, staring down into her pretty face.

Lulu tossed her head, her dark hair flowing over her shoulders in soft, touchable waves. And as she stepped closer, tempting him with the scent of her perfume, it took every ounce of self-control he had not to haul her into his arms and simply breathe her in.

"Well, I'm right in my assumption, aren't I?" she demanded. "You are planning on hiring one to help you with the three little boys."

"Yes." He intended to call a five-star service as soon as he got home and have them send someone out. Hopefully, by tomorrow evening. "I was."

"Well, I'm telling you there is no need for that," she went on sweetly, "when you have *me*, volunteering for the position."

Actually, there were a lot of reasons, Sam thought. Starting with the fact he had never really gotten over Lulu. Or the way their relationship had ended. Or the fact that, even now, he found himself wanting to take her to bed and make love to her over and over again.

Was she feeling the same damning pull of attraction? And if so, where would that lead them? "Why do you want to do this?" he asked.

She shrugged, suddenly holding back as much as he

was. She spread her hands wide. "Well, at the moment, it's not like I have anything else to do."

Uh-huh. "And if I believe that, you have some prime swampland to sell me."

"Okay." She flushed guiltily and her tongue snaked out to wet her lower lip. "You're right." A small sigh. "I do have an ulterior motive."

Now they were talking.

"I want to be there for the children in case things don't work out with the four of you."

"Except…they're going to work out, darlin'," he promised, just as persuasively.

At his assertion, an inscrutable veil slipped over her eyes. Her slender body stiffened and he took in the gentle rise and fall of her breasts.

"You seem sure of that," she said finally.

Sam nodded. Trying to keep his own latent anger and disappointment at bay, he replied, "When *I* make a commitment, Lulu, I keep it." Their eyes locked, held. Memories came flooding back.

Reminded of their falling-out all those years ago, and the reason for it, the color in her cheeks grew even rosier.

"Even if they do work out just fine with you…as their *single* daddy…you're going to need loving backup for them. And what better person for that role than their next, and *only remaining*, named legal guardian?"

She had a point. What she was suggesting did sort of make sense. At least when it came to doing what was best for the three little ones.

"You'd have to come to my ranch," he warned.

"Obviously."

"And be available to help whenever, wherever, however I need you."

He expected her to resist. Instead, she did not so much

as flinch. She rocked forward on the toes of her cowgirl boots, patient and ready. "I can make plenty of sacrifices, when necessary."

There had been a time, he thought irritably, when that wasn't the case.

"In fact, if you'll let me take charge of them, you won't even have to pay me or be anything more than an admirable father figure in their lives. I'm perfectly willing to handle everything on my own."

She was deliberately calling the shots and shutting him out. He frowned, warning her, "I intend to be a lot more hands-on than that, darlin'. And if you take this on, I will pay you the going rate."

"Okay. Well, then, if you want, I'll do the days while you're out working. When you get home at night, you could take over completely in the evening."

As much as he wanted that to be the case, he knew that might be a little much for him. Especially in the beginning, until the kids got settled in and developed a routine.

As if sensing that, she continued, "Or you could have me stay and help you until they're all in bed for the night. And then I could still head home to my place. After all…" Lulu sighed, pausing to look him in the eye, letting him know that nothing essential would ever change between the two of them, even if two-year-old triplets were involved, "…like oil and water, you and I will never really mix." She pivoted and headed for the barn. "Not for long, anyway."

We could, Sam thought, with a ferocity that surprised him, *if you would ever give us even half a chance.*

But Lulu wouldn't, he realized, watching her long legs eat up the ground. Not back then, when they had loved each other, and clearly not now, given the lingering animosity between them.

He caught up with her, overwhelmed yet again with the desire to sweep her into his arms and kiss her until she melted against him. Pushing the impulse aside, he retorted gruffly, "We need to think about what is right for the kids, Lulu." *Not what either of us wish could happen in some fantasy world.*

She shut one barn door, then the other. Over her shoulder, she sent him a contemplative look and said, "I am thinking, Sam." She brushed past him and headed for the porch of her small and tidy cottage-style home.

She settled on one of the cozy wicker chairs on the front porch. With a gesture, she invited him to make himself comfortable, too. "In fact, I haven't stopped mulling over what to do since the moment I heard about the triplets being orphaned. Which is why I know in my heart that the boys need to be here in Laramie County, where they will be well cared for and loved. Not just by you or me but by the whole community."

Sam wasn't surprised Lulu was feeling protective. She had always been sweetly maternal. An emotion that as of late had been bestowed upon her bees.

She had also switched gears pretty quickly. From cantankerous ex slash opponent, to heartbroken business owner, to ferociously determined nanny-to-be. He couldn't help but wonder if they were moving too fast, if they shouldn't ask for an extra few days to think about what they wanted to do, before they gave Hiram their answer.

Able to see how Lulu might take such a suggestion, however, he said only, "You're really willing to go all out to lend a hand, even after what happened here at the Honeybee Ranch today?" A theft that had left her devastated?

She gave him a look that said, *Especially after this.* "First of all, Sam," she reflected sadly, "we owe it to our friends to do everything we can to protect and nurture their three little boys."

Renewed grief wafted over him, too. "I agree," he said gruffly.

"Second, it'll keep me busy until I see *if* my hives will ever be recovered." As she seemed to fear they wouldn't be. "Third, to make this work, you're going to need help. Lots of it."

He leaned against a post on the porch and studied her. Aware the impulsive, reckless, romantic side of her was simultaneously the most thrilling and the most irritating. Which made him wonder just how long she would last, in what was likely to be a very challenging—and potentially heartbreaking—situation.

He sauntered toward her. "I don't half do anything, Lulu." A fact he'd made perfectly clear ten years before.

Her lower lip slid out in a delicious pout. She rose with elegant grace to face off with him. "Unlike me, I suppose?"

He let his gaze drift over her, taking in her luscious curves and lithe frame, her elegant arms and long sexy legs. "I wasn't talking about our previous big mistake."

She sent her glance heavenward. Sighed, with what seemed like enormous regret. "It was that, all right."

He jammed his hands on his waist and lowered his face to hers, wishing she had realized that a whole lot sooner. Like at the beginning of their spring break, instead of the end. "It was your idea in the first place."

She glared back at him. "Yeah, well, you went along with me, cowboy. At least initially."

Until she'd begun to panic. And suffer regret. Then, well, it had been clear their relationship was all over.

Emotion rose as their stare-down continued.

Realizing she had almost goaded him into losing his

cool, Sam shoved a hand through his hair and stepped away. Deciding it might be best to be more direct, he said honestly, "This is what worries me, darlin'. The fact we can hardly be around each other without quarreling."

Lulu nodded. Sober now. "It would worry me, too, if we didn't have something much more important to worry about. The health and welfare and happiness of Theresa and Peter's three boys."

She released a soft, empathetic sigh and compassion gleamed in her eyes. "You heard what Hiram said. They're at the end of the line of the named guardians. If we don't want them to end up separated and in foster care, you and I are going to *have* to find a way to make it all work." She paused to draw a deep, enervating breath that lifted the curves of her breasts against her polo shirt. "I don't think, under the circumstances, that this is too much to ask of us. Do you? Especially since Peter and Theresa named both of us in their wills?"

"All right," Sam said, deciding he could be as selfless as she was being and more. "I'll agree to this arrangement for one month." *Which should be enough time for you to realize how unworkable a situation this is going to be for the two of us, and then decide to simply take on the role of close family friend.* "At the end of that time," he said sternly, "we reassess. And if we need to find a professional nanny, we will."

"Agreed. Although I have to warn you, I'm not going to change my mind."

That, Sam thought, remained to be seen. From what he'd observed, one two-year-old could be a lot. Three... at one time...who were also in mourning...? But in the short-term, there were other important things they needed to worry about, too. Her personal safety being paramount.

"Where are you going to be this evening?" he asked,

guessing she hadn't yet told her family what had happened. Otherwise her cell phone would have been ringing off the hook and the place would have been inundated with McCabes.

But they would know, as soon as the ranchers in the family got the alert from the cattleman's association. "Are you going to stay with your parents?"

She blinked, confused. "Why would I want to do that?"

"In case the rustlers come back."

She pooh-poohed the notion, fearless as always. "They already took everything of value."

She had a point. They hadn't touched her house. And they certainly could have looted it, too, if they had wanted to do so. Still... He gazed down at her. "I think until we know more about who did this and why, you'll be safer elsewhere, Lulu."

"And I think I'll be just fine right here." She took hold of his biceps and steered him toward the porch steps, clearly done with this topic.

But he was not satisfied. Not in the least. Because the need to protect her was back, stronger than ever. "Lulu..."

She peered up at him from beneath a fringe of dark lashes. "You just worry about contacting Hiram and getting the triplets here as soon as possible. I'll handle the rest." She went into the house and shut the door behind her.

Chapter Three

"Sam's *still* out there?" Lulu's mother, Rachel, asked during the impromptu family phone call an hour later.

Grimacing, Lulu peeked out the window of her living room, catching a glimpse of the ornery cowboy through the dusky light. Cell phone still pressed to her ear, she confirmed, "He's sitting in his pickup truck, talking on the phone and doing something on what appears to be a laptop." Looking as devastatingly handsome and sexy as ever with his hat tossed off and his sleeves rolled up, another button of his shirt undone. Not that she was noticing the effect the summer heat might be having on him...

"Good for him," growled her father. He had heard all about the theft from other members of the cattleman's association before she'd even managed to call home to tell them. "Since Sam obviously doesn't think you should be left alone right now, either."

But Sam had once, Lulu thought. When the two of

them had been at odds, he'd had no problem issuing an ultimatum. When he'd become deeply disappointed in her and walked away.

"Now, Frank," her mother warned, "Lulu can make her own decisions."

On the other end of the connection, her father har-rumphed.

Lulu didn't want what she saw as her problems bringing conflict to her family. "It's not that I don't appreciate the offers made by you and my brothers," she said soothingly. All five of whom wanted to help out by either temporarily taking her into their home or standing guard over her and her property. "It's just that I need some alone time right now."

She needed time to think, to figure out how she and Sam were going to manage the triplets. Without continually bringing up any of their former angst.

With uncanny intuition, her mother asked, "Is there anything else going on?"

Glad she had opted not to FaceTime or speak with her parents in person, at least not until after Sam had formally become the triplets' guardian and she their nanny, Lulu tensed. "Like what?" She feigned innocence. Knowing her folks, they were going to have a lot of opinions about her decision to become a parent this way, too.

"I'm not sure." Her mother paused.

Lulu's heartbeat accelerated as she saw Sam get out of his pickup truck and stride through the twilight. He still had his cell phone and a laptop in his big hands. "Listen, Mom, Dad, I've gotta go. Talk to you soon." She hung up before they had a chance to reply.

The doorbell rang.

Her body thrumming with a mixture of impatience and anticipation, she switched on the porch light and opened the door. She stood, blocking him, and gave him a deadpan look. "Yes?"

His legs were braced apart, broad shoulders squared. Looking as confident and determined as ever, he turned his ruggedly handsome face to hers. "I wanted to tell you what the cattlemen have unearthed thus far," he said in the low, masculine voice she knew so well.

Lulu blinked in surprise and glanced at her watch. "It's only been a few hours."

A stubble of evening beard, a shade darker than his wheat-blond hair, lined his jaw. A matter-of-fact smile turned up the corners of his sensual lips. But it was the compelling intensity of his eyes that unraveled her every time. No matter how fiercely she determined that he would not get to her. Not again. "When it comes to rustlers, it's important to strike before the trail gets cold," he explained.

She couldn't argue that.

Their eyes met for one brief, telling moment, that—however fleeting—had them on the exact same page.

Gratitude oozing through her and figuring they might as well sit down for this, she ushered him in. He followed her past the cozy seating area and over to the kitchen island, where she'd been working on her own laptop, notifying fellow beekeepers of what had transpired.

Sam set his belongings down but remained standing. "First," he said, "I want to tell you that I phoned Hiram and told him you and I were going to be jointly caring for the boys, at least in the interim. Me as their permanent legal guardian, you as their nanny. He was on board with the idea of the two of us joining forces during the kids' transition, so the triplets are being brought to my ranch tomorrow afternoon around 3:30 p.m."

Wow, Sam worked fast. On multiple fronts. But then

he always had. His ability to really get things done was one of the things she admired most about him.

He paused to check an incoming text on his phone, then turned his attention back to her. "Apparently, they are going to have everything they need with them for the short-term, and the rest of their belongings will be delivered by movers the following day."

She nodded, trying not to think about how attracted to him she still was.

His gaze roving her head to toe, he continued, "So, if you would like to be at Hidden Creek with me to greet them…"

There were times when he made her feel very comfortable, and then there were others, like now, when he made her feel very off-kilter. Lulu moved around to the other side of the island. "I would." She busied herself, putting a few dishes away.

He smiled. "Great. And second of all…" He settled his six-foot-three-inch frame on the bar stool, opened up his laptop and, eyes locked on hers, continued, "I know that you gave some of this information to the sheriff's department regarding the theft, but I want to make sure I didn't miss anything, if that's okay."

Ribbons of sensation ghosting down her spine, Lulu dipped her head in assent. He nodded back at her, then typed in a few words. "The burglary happened sometime this morning."

His manner was so businesslike, Lulu began to realize she could lean on Sam, at least in this situation, if only she allowed herself to do so.

Determined to keep him at arm's length, she fought the waves of sexual magnetism that always existed between them. "Sometime between eight o'clock, when I left for town to set up my lunch service for my food truck," she confirmed. "And when the sheriff's department notified me at around five o'clock, to let me know there had been a break-in."

Which left a huge nine-hour window.

His big hands paused over the keys. "A customer reported it?"

Aware she was suddenly feeling shaky again, Lulu moved around the island in search of a place to sit down. "Lucille Lockhart came out to buy some honey. She hadn't read my social media page advertising the location of my food truck today, so she didn't know I wasn't here." But the thieves likely had.

Sam made a low, thoughtful sound. "And everything was gone when Mrs. Lockhart arrived?"

She settled in the high-backed stool next to him and swiveled to face him. The sincerity in his gaze was almost as unnerving as his unexpected, unrelenting kindness. "The entire apiary was emptied, and so were the storehouse shelves. Panic-stricken, Mrs. Lockhart tried to call me, and when she couldn't reach me, she notified the sheriff. We don't know much more than that right now."

"Actually, we do." He swiveled toward her, too, and braced one elbow on the counter next to his laptop. His other hand rested on his rock-hard thigh. Nodding tersely once again, he added, "I put out the word when we got here. I've heard back from almost all our members."

She caught her breath at the worry in his eyes.

"Apparently two trucks were spotted on the farm-to-market road that goes by here around one o'clock this afternoon. They seemed to be traveling together and were headed north. One was a white refrigeration truck, the other a flatbed loaded with two off-road forklifts." His lips compressed, and his gruff tone registered his disappointment. "We didn't get an actual license number, but someone noticed the plates were from Wisconsin."

Hope mingling with dread, Lulu laid her hand across her heart. "They're sure it was a refrigeration truck?"

"It had the cooling unit on top of the cab."

Relief filtered through her. She didn't know whether to shout hallelujah or sob with relief. In truth, she felt like doing both. "Oh, thank heavens," she whispered finally.

"That's important?" Sam guessed.

Lulu swallowed around the ache in her throat. "Very. The bees wouldn't survive in their boxes if they were transported a long way in this kind of heat." She ran her hand over the side seam of her denim skirt. Sam's glance followed her reflexive move. Realizing the fabric had ridden up, Lulu did her best to surreptitiously tug it down. Yet, maddeningly, the hem remained several inches above her bare knees.

Knees he had once caressed with devastating sensuality.

Pushing aside her rush of self-consciousness, she added, "Moving bees is hard on them as it is."

Sam lifted his glance and locked eyes with her yet again. He regarded her with the respect of a fellow rancher. "Makes sense they'd do better if they were kept cool." He rubbed his jaw. "That kind of truck will also make the thieves easier to find."

Glad he had taken it upon himself to help her, even when she had preferred he leave her to handle everything on her own, Lulu drew a breath. It would be so easy to lean on him again. Too easy, maybe, given how acrimoniously they had once parted. "So what now?" she asked quietly.

Sam sobered, the corners of his lips slanting down. "I've already notified the sheriff's department with all the information I was able to compile, and they in turn have put out an APB and will be checking with truck stops and weighing stations for any vehicles fitting the description."

Feeling her first concrete ray of hope, Lulu asked, "You really think we might find them?"

He nodded. "Trucks like that can't stick to country roads without drawing a lot of attention. On the highway, they'll be a lot easier to find. Hopefully, we'll know something soon."

He shut the lid on his laptop and stood.

Feeling surprisingly reluctant to see him go, Lulu rose, too. "Sam..." She touched his arm, delaying him. He turned to gaze down at her and her heart rate kicked up another notch.

"I really... I don't know how to thank you," she continued sincerely. "A few hours ago, I had very little hope I'd ever see my beehives again. Now, well." She struggled to put her gratitude into words. As she gazed up at him, she pushed through the wealth of conflicting emotions suddenly racing through her and tried again. "I never would have expected you to...help."

Something dark and turbulent flashed in his eyes. "Well, you should have," he said, as if fighting his own inner demons.

The next thing Lulu knew, she was all the way in his arms. His head was lowering, his lips capturing hers. His kiss was everything she remembered, everything she had ever dreamed of receiving, everything the wildly impulsive and romantic part of her still wanted.

From him...

Because the truth was, no one had ever affected her like Sam did. No one had ever made her want, wish, need... And as his lips ravished hers, she moaned at the sweet, enervating heat. The touch of his tongue against hers sent her even further over the edge. Wreathing her arms about his neck, she shifted closer. Nestling the softness of her breasts against the solid, unyielding warmth of his broad chest. His hand swept lower, bringing her even nearer. And, just like that, the walls she'd erected around her began to crumble and her heart expanded, tenfold.

One kiss melded into another. And then another…and another. Until he had her surrendering to the firm, insistent pressure of his mouth as never before. She clung to him, soaking up everything about him. His strength, his scent. His warmth and tenderness. Years of pent-up emotion poured out of her as she rose on tiptoe and pressed her body even closer against the hardness of his.

And still he kissed her. Slowly and thoroughly. Softly and sweetly. With building need. Until a low, helpless moan escaped her throat. And she recalled everything that had once brought them together…and had ultimately torn them apart…

Sam hadn't meant to kiss her. Hadn't thought he would even come close. But when Lulu had looked up at him with such sweet surprise in her expression, well, it triggered something in him. Something primitive and hot and wild.

It had made him want to claim her again.

As his woman.

As his…

He cut off the thought before it could fully form. Knowing there was no way either of them could go back to that tumultuous period of time, even if the hot, intense connection that had always been between them was definitely still there. And she knew it, too, as he felt her begin to tense the way she always did when she began to have second thoughts.

With a sigh, he drew back. Sure of what he was going to see.

She gazed up at him, eyes awash with the kind of turbulent emotion that had always signaled trouble for them. Lower lip trembling, she flattened her hands over his chest and pushed him away. "We can't do this again."

And once again, the need to possess her got the better of his common sense.

"Why not?" he demanded gruffly.

"Because we already proved it will never work between us," she whispered, the shimmering hurt back in her pretty eyes, "and I really don't want to go there again."

To Lulu's relief, after a moment's consideration, Sam seemed to concede it wouldn't be wise to complicate their situation any further.

And when he greeted her at the door of his sprawling ranch house the following afternoon, his manner was appropriately circumspect.

Which left her free to forget about the heady aftermath of their passionate embrace and concentrate on the changes made to the Hidden Creek cattle ranch since she had last been there.

The thousand-acre spread was as tidy and filled with good-looking cattle as ever, the barns, stables, bunkhouse and other buildings meticulously well kept. He had updated the main house with dark gray paint on the brick, white trim and black shutters. She admired the beautifully landscaped front lawn and the circular drive directing guests to the covered porch and inviting front door. A quartet of dormer windows adorned the steeply pitched roof.

Most arresting of all, though, was the ruggedly handsome rancher who ushered her inside. The corners of his sensual lips lifted in an appraising smile. He came close enough she could smell the soap and sun and man scent of his skin. "A little early, aren't you?"

Her heart panged in her chest. "I wanted to make sure I was here when they arrived, but if you'd like me to wait in my SUV…" Aware she was fast becoming a bundle of nerves, she gestured at the Lexus in the driveway.

"Don't be ridiculous." He ushered her inside.

Aware the atmosphere between them was quickly becoming highly charged and way too intimate, Lulu turned her attention elsewhere. There'd been a lot of changes since she'd been here last, she noted as she followed him. The ecru walls and dark wide-plank wood floors were the same, but the fancy upholstered pieces and heavy custom draperies favored by his late mother had been exchanged for large leather couches, mahogany furniture and modern plantation shutters. A lot of the knickknacks and elegant paintings were gone, replaced by a handsomely redone white brick fireplace and mantel, a complete wall of built-in bookshelves and a state-of-the-art entertainment center.

His gaze dropped to the hamper in her hand "Planning a picnic?" he drawled.

Lulu's hands curled around the wicker handle. "I'm open to whatever the kids need, although I don't really know what to expect when they do arrive." Which was one of the reasons she was so uncharacteristically on edge.

Evidently that was something they had in common. Sam sighed. "Me, either." He led the way down the hall to the back of the ranch house, where changes also abounded. The kitchen's flowered wallpaper and frilly curtains were gone, replaced by stainless steel appliances and concrete countertops and sleek white walls washed in sunlight. The breakfast room table and eight captain chairs were the same, although all had been refinished with a glowing golden-oak stain. The family room had become a work space, with file cabinets, a U-shaped computer desk, scanner/copier phone and printer.

He squinted at her. "Meet your approval?"

With effort, she met his probing gaze. She set the hamper on the island—also new—in the center of the large square kitchen. "It's very nice. You've outdone yourself," she said.

He shrugged, all affable male again. "Can't take all the credit. My sister Lainey is an interior designer now, so she helped. Tara, the computer expert, set up all my business systems for me. Liza, the chef, taught me how to cook. Betsy, the innkeeper, showed me how to properly stock a pantry and freezer."

Like the McCabes, the Kirklands always had each other's backs. "Your sisters are scattered all over now, aren't they?"

"Yep." He lounged against the counter, arms folded. "I'm the only one left in Texas."

Trying not to notice how well he filled out his ranching clothes, she asked, "You miss them?"

His gaze skimmed her appreciatively. "They visit."

Not an answer. But then, he had never been one to own up to anything that hurt. He just moved on.

As he was about to do now...

He inclined his head. "So what's in there?" he asked.

"I wasn't sure what you had on hand or what they were sending with the kids, so I brought some toddler favorites like applesauce and kid-friendly mac and cheese for their dinner, just in case."

Another nod. "Thanks," he said, as a big, sleepy-looking Saint Bernard came around the corner. The brown patches of fur over the pet's eyes and back and chest contrasted with the fluffy white coat everywhere else. An extremely feminine flowered pink collar encircled her neck.

Lulu watched the big dog pad gracefully over to stand beside Sam. She sat down next to him, pressing her body up against his sinewy leg and hip. Tail wagging, she gazed up at Sam adoringly. Waited, until he petted her head, then let out a long, luxuriant sigh that Lulu understood all too well.

Pushing aside the memory of Sam's gentle, soothing touch, she asked, "Who is this?"

"Beauty. As in *Beauty and the Beast*."

Unable to resist, Lulu guessed, "And you're the Beast?"

Although he tried, he couldn't quite contain a smile. "Very funny."

Lulu chuckled. "I thought so."

Although, the moniker fit. The 120-pound dog was absolutely gorgeous. And not really the type of canine she would have expected a rough-hewn rancher like Sam to choose.

"When did you get her?" Lulu smiled and made eye contact with Beauty, who appreciated her right back.

Tilting his head, Sam paused, calculating. "A little over four years ago."

"As a puppy?"

"She was about six months old at the time."

Lulu paused. "I didn't know you wanted a dog." He certainly hadn't mentioned it when they were together.

Back then, all he'd talked about were horses and cattle. And of course the importance of keeping one's commitments. Which he definitely did not think Lulu had done.

He smiled as his dog stood again and then stretched her front legs out in front of her, dipping her tummy close to the floor in a play bow. "She's not mine. She belongs to my sister Hailey."

Hence, the romantic pet name.

Lulu turned back to him, confused. "But...you're keeping her?" She watched Beauty rise again and turn back to Sam for one last pet on the head.

His big hand sank into the soft, luxuriant fur on the top of Beauty's head, massaging it lightly in a way that made Lulu's own nerve endings shudder and her mouth go dry.

"It was never the intention," Sam admitted, oblivious to the effect his tender ministrations were having on Lulu. "But Beauty was too big for Hailey's apartment, and she suddenly had to travel internationally for her job. Constantly boarding Beauty didn't seem fair. My sister asked me to help out temporarily, since I have plenty of room. I agreed."

Lulu observed the free-flowing affection between man and pet. "Looks like you made the right decision."

And possibly, Lulu thought as Beauty lumbered over to stand next to her, the right decision regarding the three kids, as well.

Because if Sam wouldn't turn out a dog who had come to live with him, she knew he would never abandon three little orphaned boys. And that meant if she was going to form a permanent, loving connection with Theresa and Peter's triplets, she would have to forget the difficulties of their past and find a way to forge an enduring, *platonic* connection with Sam, too.

The next twenty minutes passed with excruciating

slowness. Sam settled down to do something at his desk while Lulu paced, looking out one front window, then the next.

Finally, a large dark green van made its way up the lane. It stopped next to the ranch house. The doors opened. Hiram Higgins and three other adults stepped out. And even though there was no sign of the children they were going to care for just yet, Lulu's heartbeat quickened.

"Sam! They're here!" she exclaimed.

He rose and strode briskly through the hall to her side.

Together, they walked out the front door and down the porch steps. Hiram introduced his wife, Winnifred, a kind-faced woman with gray hair, and Sandra and Jim Kelleher, the thirtysomething couple who had been looking after the triplets.

Seeing that Lulu and Sam were chomping at the bit to meet the kids, the Kellehers proceeded to unfasten safety harnesses and bring the children out, one by one. All three were holding stuffed animals and clutching well-loved blue baby blankets. In deference to the shimmering June heat, they were wearing blue plaid shorts and coordinating T-shirts, sandals, plaid bucket hats and kiddie sunglasses. All appeared shy and maybe even a little dazed. As if they'd been napping and were still trying to wake up.

"This is Theo," Winnifred introduced the most serious-looking toddler.

Sandra brought forward the one with the trembling lower lip. "And Ethan."

"And Andrew," Jim said, shifting the weight of the only one starting to fidget.

"Hello, Theo, Ethan and Andrew," Lulu greeted them in turn.

They simply stared at her, then eventually turned away.

Her heart sank. She was a McCabe. She'd been around children all her life. Not once had one responded to her with such indifference.

But then, these children had been through hell. It was probably no surprise they'd become...numb.

Hiram retrieved his briefcase and inclined his head at Sam. "We probably should sign the papers first and then unload the belongings they brought with them today."

"Lulu," Sam said, "you want to take them all on in?"

"Sure." She led the way inside as Sam and Hiram adjourned to a corner of the front porch. Winnifred and the Kellehers took a seat in the living area, a child on each lap. Once they were all settled, Lulu sat down, too, and they got down to business.

"I brought a folder with me of everything I've been able to piece together about the children's previous routines, plus everything that did or did not work for us, in terms of their care," Sandra said.

Jim exhaled, then turned to look at Lulu. "I hope Sam has better luck with them. It's good you're going to be helping out, too."

Winnifred chimed in, "Hiram and I can both attest to that. They can be a handful."

Suddenly feeling a little unsure they were up to the task, Lulu nodded her understanding. Had she and Sam underestimated the task of helping the orphaned triplets?

Sam and Hiram walked in. After Sam set the papers on the entry table, Jim handed the still-fidgety Andrew to Lulu and all three men headed back outside. Short minutes later, a trio of car seats, travel beds, booster seats, suitcases, and a big box of toys were stacked in a corner of the living room.

"Probably best we be on our way," Hiram said.

Lulu expected the kids to wail in protest at the impending departure of yet another set of guardians. Instead, they took it stoically in stride. Too stoically, in fact, to be believed.

Chapter Four

"How long do you think they're going to sit there like that, before they decide to get comfy and stay awhile?" Sam quipped to Lulu a good half hour later. Although he was the one with legal responsibility for them, she was the one who seemed to inherently understand what was going on with them. That put them all in the awkward position of really needing her soothing maternal presence in a way Sam hadn't expected. And that he wasn't sure how to deal with, given his ever-present desire for her.

Oblivious to his chaotic thoughts, Lulu looked up from the toy fort she was building in the center of the living room floor and turned her glance in the direction Sam indicated.

The triplets were right where they'd initially settled. Cuddled together in the middle of his big leather sofa. All still wore their hats and sunglasses. Their blankets and stuffed animals were on their laps. Thumbs in their mouths. All previous attempts, and there had been three thus far, to gently separate them from their head-wear had failed.

"I don't know." With a shrug, Lulu continued pulling toys from the box. Unlike him, she was completely at ease, despite the fact that, like him, she'd been rebuffed at every attempt to get acquainted with the children, too. Her turquoise eyes sparkled with amusement and her soft lips curved into a sweet, contented smile. "Until they're ready to do something else?"

Sam edged closer and caught a whiff of her signature fragrance. With effort, he concentrated on the problem at hand. Helping the boys acclimate.

"With those sunglasses on, this place has to look dark to them, even though we opened up the blinds and turned the lights on." He wondered if they were scared.

Lulu dusted off her hands and stood. Looking incredibly fetching in a pretty floral sundress and casual canvas flats, she came close enough to go up on tiptoe and whisper in his ear, "Would you relax, cowboy?" Her hand curved over his biceps. "I think your anxiety is making them tense."

Was it his imagination or was it getting hot in here? "I'm not anxious."

Clearly, she didn't believe him.

She let go of him for a moment and stepped back to study him from beneath a fringe of thick, dark lashes, then lightly clasped one of his forearms just above his wrist. "Let's just give them a moment to acclimate without us staring at them, okay?" She gave a little tug when he didn't budge. "Come on. You can help me set their booster seats up at the kitchen table. Maybe set out a snack or…" she glanced at her watch, noting that it was nearly five o'clock "…dinner."

Her soft skin feeling like a silky manacle around his

wrist, she guided him down the wide hallway to the kitchen. Sam pushed away the evocative memories her touch engendered. Exhaled. For once, he was all too willing to let her be in charge of what went on with the two of them. In fact, the knowledge that she had some idea of what to do was reassuring.

His sisters had done all the babysitting when they were growing up. Not him. And the truth was, he had no idea at all how to handle a situation like this.

Sam peeked back into the living room, far enough to be able to surreptitiously check on the three little boys and see they were just where they had been.

Then he moved back toward Lulu. Stood, back braced against the kitchen island, feet crossed at the ankle, arms folded. "You think they're hungry?"

She ran a hand through her sun-streaked honey brown hair, pushing the silky waves off her face. As she squared her shoulders, the luscious curves of her breasts pushed against the bodice of her dress. "I'm sure they are. Thirsty, too." She removed three small cartons of apple juice and a container of Goldfish crackers from the bag, then set them all on the counter.

"I also know they've had a very rough time, being shuffled from home to home for the last two months." She paused to look into Sam's eyes. "They've got to be very confused."

He let his gaze drift over her, surprised at how good it felt to have her here, in his home, with him. When all they'd done for years was try to stay as far apart from each other as possible. He was beginning to see what a mistake that was. Clearly, there was a lot of unfinished business between them. Aware they were definitely on the same page about one thing—making the triplets happy again—he murmured, "I want them to feel good about being here."

"I'm sure they will," she reassured him softly. "But we have to give them time, Sam."

Without warning, Beauty, who'd been sleeping on her cushion in the corner of the kitchen, lifted her head. Got to her feet. And ever so slowly moved toward the hall.

Wondering what the Saint Bernard had heard, Sam turned in that direction.

There it was.

The unmistakable sound of childlike chatter.

Lulu started in surprise. Pausing to give him a quick, excited glance, she tiptoed down the hallway toward the living room. Sam was right on her heels, moving just as soundlessly.

And there they were. All three boys. Finally sans bucket hats and sunglasses, sitting on the floor, in the middle of their toys.

"You were right," Sam murmured, standing close enough to feel the heat emanating from her slender body. "All we needed to do was give them a little room to maneuver."

Lulu nodded, although to his consternation she didn't look nearly as relieved as he felt to see them up and about.

Figuring it was his turn to comfort her, he reached over to give her forearm a companionable squeeze. "Maybe acclimating them won't be so difficult after all," he theorized.

Except as it turned out, Lulu noted in despair many times over the next eight hours, it absolutely was.

The three boys all refused their snack, and, except for a few sips of their apple juice, also made a mess of their dinner. Squishing the mac and cheese between their fingers and smearing it on their plates and the table in front of them. Banana slices, applesauce and chopped green beans shared a similar fate. In fact, once they'd finished, it looked as if there had been one heck of a food fight in Sam's kitchen.

Once down from the table, they began to run and climb and shout, while Beauty lay on the floor, watching over them with a sweet maternal grace. As if the Saint Bernard knew exactly what they were thinking and feeling.

Which was good, Lulu thought with increasing disquiet. Because neither she nor Sam had a clue. A fact that really hit home when she decided to take matters in hand and put the overtired little munchkins to bed.

Her old camp-counselor smile plastered on her face, Lulu approached the boys. "Guess what, fellas?" she said. "It's almost bedtime."

"That's right, bedtime," Sam echoed cheerfully.

"Nooooo!" all three boys yelled in unison, then went racing off in all directions.

Sam and Lulu leaped into action. He plucked Andrew off the top of the sofa, then intercepted Ethan, who was scurrying up the stairs to the second floor. Meanwhile, Lulu scooped Theo into her arms before he could reach the remotes on the third shelf of the entertainment center. "Who wants to take a bubble bath?" she asked, even more enthusiastically.

Theo wriggled like a tadpole in Lulu's arms. "No bath!" he shouted.

Ethan and Andrew echoed the sentiment as Sam lowered them onto the living room floor. Lulu followed suit with Theo.

The mania increased.

Sam looked over at her, clearly at wit's end. "We have to do something," he said firmly.

Lulu struggled to catch her breath while the boys began doing somersaults in the middle of the rug. "Agreed."

"Then…?"

She knew she was the one with all the childcare experience, from her high school and college days. But even some of the most difficult situations at summer camp had never been like this. No wonder none of the other guardians had been able to handle the triplets.

"Maybe we should pass on the baths and just put them in clean diapers and pajamas before starting the bedtime routine," she said.

He nodded, clearly ready to comply with anything she suggested. Which was unusual. He generally liked to be in charge.

"Got anything to bribe them with?" she asked.

His broad shoulders lifted in an amiable shrug. "Cookies?"

"Worth a try!"

He disappeared and came back with a transparent bakery container. "Who wants a chocolate chip cookie?" he said, holding it aloft.

The boys stopped.

Lulu could see they were about to refuse this, too.

Sam lowered the container so they could get a better look at the confections inside.

Three thumbs immediately went into mouths. They were thinking. Checking with each other silently. Considering.

Good. "All you have to do," Lulu coaxed, "is get ready for bed. Then you can have a cookie *and* a bedtime story. Maybe even a glass of milk, okay?"

The triplets stood still.

Being careful not to spook them, she got out the necessary items, and with Sam's help, swiftly got them all changed. When all were ready, Sam doled out the cookies as promised.

The three of them climbed up onto the center of the sofa and began to chomp away. While Sam watched over them, Lulu raced into the kitchen and brought back three sippy cups of milk.

One by one, they drank that, too.

Pleased she and Sam had been able to work together to bring peace to the household, Lulu smiled. Indicating Sam should take one end of the sofa, she slipped onto the other and began to read a story that—from the well-worn condition of it—appeared to be one of their favorites. It was about a dog who went into his little house to find shelter from the storm and was soon joined by every other animal nearby. By the time the storm passed, the doghouse was full. New friendships had been formed. And everyone was still safe and warm and happy.

As she hoped they would soon be here, at Hidden Creek.

"Would you like another story?" Lulu asked as the triplets blinked sleepily and their heads began to droop.

To her disappointment, there were no nods of agreement.

But no shouts of outright refusal, either. So taking that for a yes, Lulu grabbed another book and then another and another. By the time she hit the fifth story, all three toddlers were sound asleep.

Sam, who'd been hanging out simply listening, gestured toward the three carrying cases in the foyer. "Where do you think I should set up their travel beds?" he whispered.

That was easy, Lulu thought, already thinking about how hard it was going to be to say good-night this evening. But she and Sam had a deal, so...

She drew a deep, bolstering breath. "Close to you, in case they wake up."

He paused, blond brow furrowing. "I know our agreement," he said. "But...are you sure you can't stay? At least for tonight?"

The truth was, Lulu had been hoping like crazy that he'd ask. Partly because she didn't want to leave the boys, given the highly agitated state they'd been in. And also because she wasn't any more confident Sam could handle this on his own than he was.

"I'll have to run home and get a few things," she said, doing her best to hide her elation.

He nodded his assent and rose as she walked over to get her bag. Then, stepping closer, murmured in the same tender tone he had used before, "Think we should get them settled into their beds first?"

Her body tingling at his nearness, she shook her head. "I'd let them get a little deeper into sleep first."

"Okay."

Another silence fell.

He looked so momentarily unsure of himself, her heart went out to him. So she moved in to give him a quick, reassuring hug. "I know we've had a rough start today, but it's all going to work out, Sam," she promised fiercely.

"I know," he whispered back. His arms went around her and he pulled her in close, one hand idly moving down her back, reflexively calming her, too. She sank into his warmth and his strength, wishing things were as simple as they once had been. When need...want...love... were the only things driving them. But they were different people now. She needed to remember that.

Forcing herself to do what was best for all of them, Lulu drew a breath and stepped back from the enticing circle of his arms. She flashed a confident smile she couldn't begin to feel—not when it came to the two of them, anyway.

"I'll be right back," she promised. And while she was gone, for the sake of everyone, she would do her best to get her own feelings in order.

Two hours later, Sam was feeling much better. Lulu had returned with an overnight bag, honey-grilled chicken sandwiches for their dinner and the makings for a pancake breakfast the next morning. He'd cleaned up the kitchen and breakfast room and set up the three toddler travel beds in the master bedroom upstairs in her absence.

Now, with their own hunger sated, all they had to do was figure out how to move the still-snoozing tykes from the sofa to the travel beds on the second floor.

"Want me to go first?" Lulu asked as they stood shoulder to shoulder, gazing down at their little charges.

Doing his best to contain all he was feeling, Sam nodded. "I'll follow your lead."

With an adeptness Sam well remembered, Lulu eased in to remove Theo first. He was sleeping half on Ethan and had one leg beneath Andrew. She slid her hands beneath him, careful as could be not to disturb the other two. Theo shifted and sighed as she lifted him into her arms and then situated him with his head on her shoulder, his body against her middle.

"Wish me luck," she mouthed and glided off toward the stairs.

When she'd made it all the way up without incident, Sam copied her movements and eased Ethan into his arms. The little boy stirred and sighed but did not wake as Sam headed up the stairs. Slowly, he went down the hall, then into the master bedroom where Lulu was still bent over one of the travel cribs, tucking Theo in. She helped him ease Ethan down, and together, they went back to get Andrew. He slept through the move to bed, too.

Ten minutes later, all was set.

They tiptoed into the upstairs hallway. Lulu looked at him in question.

"Take any guest room you want," he said.

She chose the one two doors down. Which was probably an effort to put a little more physical space between them, since the bedroom she passed over, with a queen-size bed and adjoining bath, was almost identical.

When she turned to glance up at him, she looked tired, vulnerable and very much in need of a hug. But a hug would lead to a kiss, and a kiss would lead to everything they didn't need right now.

An electric silence fell between them and his heart kicked against his ribs.

"You'll let me know if you need me?" she said finally.

I need you now, more than I ever thought I would. He returned her half smile, promising, just as kindly, "No question."

Aware there was nothing else to say, he went back down the stairs and retrieved her overnight bag for her. They said good-night quickly, and both turned in.

Sam had no idea if Lulu fell asleep right away or not. He lay there for a while, thinking about all the mistakes they had made, everything they'd lost. How good it had felt to kiss her again the night before.

Still thinking about that, he drifted off. And it was shortly after that when the crying started. First Ethan, then Theo and Andrew.

Heart pounding, Sam threw back the covers and raced over to the travel cribs at the foot of his bed. All three boys were sitting up, distraught, rubbing their eyes.

Lulu rushed in, clad in a pair of blue-and-white-striped linen pajama pants, her hair gloriously mussed. In that instant, giving Sam an insight into what kind of mother she would be, she tenderly scooped up one child.

He reached down and lifted the other two.

"Hush now, baby, it's all right," she cooed, over and over. As did he.

To no avail. The crying continued in concert, long into the night. Sam's only comfort was the fact that Lulu was right there with them, steadfastly weathering the storm.

Chapter Five

Lulu woke slowly, aware of three things. She was incredibly exhausted, curiously weighed down, at least in the region of her midriff, and was that Sam…in all his early-morning glory…sleeping next to her? With two toddlers in his arms?

She blinked. And blinked again.

Yes, it was Sam, clad in a pair of pajama pants and a V-necked T-shirt. With his hair adorably rumpled and a morning beard rimming his chiseled jaw, he looked incredibly masculine and sexy. He was also sound asleep, his breathing as deep and even as that of the two little boys curled up on his chest, their heads nestled between his neck and shoulders.

Better yet, she had a tyke in her arms, too, snuggled up close, his head tucked between her head and shoulder. And all five of them were cozied up in Sam's king-size bed.

Without warning, he stirred slightly. Drew a deep, bolstering breath and opened his eyes.

He turned to look at her, his lips curving up in that sleepy-sexy, good-morning way she recalled so well.

Contentment roared through her, making her feel all warm and cozy inside.

His glance roved her slowly. It seemed like he might be feeling some of that contentment, too. "Some night, huh?" he murmured huskily.

It had been. The boys had cried off and on for hours. Every time they thought they had one asleep, another woke him.

The only thing that had soothed any of them was being walked. And so they'd roamed the master bedroom, crooning softly, Lulu with one toddler in her arms, Sam with two in his.

Until finally, around four in the morning, the boys had drifted off, and wary of disturbing them yet again, Sam and Lulu had eased onto the center of his big bed, children still in their arms. They lay there gently, daring to relax fully and close their eyes. And then, finally, slept.

Admiration shone in Sam's eyes. "You were great with them last night," he said.

She knew the memory of the boys' first night would stick with her. "So were you…"

Theo snuggled close, yawned sleepily, squirmed again and then lifted his head. Andrew and Ethan swiftly followed suit. All looked expectantly in the direction of the open bedroom door. "Mommy?" Theo said.

"Daddy?" Andrew asked.

"Go home?" Ethan demanded.

The plaintive requests, along with the confusion and lack of comprehension in the boys' eyes, tugged on Lulu's heartstrings and filled her with sorrow. She mourned Peter and Theresa, too. She could only imagine how poignant the loss was for the boys. No wonder they were out of control. They didn't understand where their parents were. And at their young age, there was no way to explain.

Her vision blurred.

Sam cleared his throat. "Mommy and Daddy are in heaven," he said gently. "But you know who we do have?" He indicated the stuffed animals scattered around them. "Tiger and Elephant and Giraffe!"

Grinning, the boys picked up their stuffed animals and clutched them to their chests.

"And blankets, too!" Sam declared.

They grabbed those, as well.

Her heart aching with an emotion that was almost primal in its intensity, Lulu did her best to smile, too, and affect an air of normalcy. Her grieving would have to come later, privately. "How about we all go downstairs and I'll rustle up some breakfast?" she suggested.

Sam reached over and squeezed her shoulder. Although the boys' hurt and confusion had affected him, too, he had regained his composure swiftly. "Sounds like a plan to me…"

Sam had to hand it to Lulu. Even though he could see her heart was breaking for the boys, as was his, she pulled it together with feminine grace. Helped with the three diaper changes and, along with Beauty who'd been sleeping on the floor of his bedroom as per usual, escorted the boys downstairs.

While the triplets played with their toys in the living room, she went into the kitchen to start breakfast. He let Beauty outside and put on a pot of coffee. She was still dressed in blue-and-white-striped pajama pants and a white scoop-necked T-shirt that nicely outlined her slender body. Her dark hair was tousled, her cheeks pink with sleep, her turquoise eyes red-rimmed with fatigue.

He cupped a hand over her shoulder as she passed, temporarily stilling her. "Hey. If you want to go back to bed for a while…"

She pivoted another quarter turn, so she was looking up at him directly. Acting as if that were the most ridiculous suggestion she had ever heard, she wrinkled her nose at him. "Ah, no."

"Sure?" he pressed. Aware he was still holding onto her, dropped his hand. Filled with the surprising urge to protect her, too, he said, "You only got two or three hours of sleep."

Propping one hand on her hip, she looked him over, head to toe. "Which, as it turns out, was exactly what you and the boys got," she retorted. "Seriously." Her gaze gentled. "I'm fine. I want to be available to the kids whenever, however they need me."

Before he could respond, the doorbell rang.

"Expecting someone?" she asked.

"No." Sam went to get the door while Lulu remained in the kitchen.

A uniformed Laramie County sheriff's deputy was on his doorstep. And not just any deputy, but Lulu's brother, Dan.

He touched the brim of his hat in an official manner, the grim look in his eyes indicating that although they were longtime acquaintances, this was not a social call. "Sam," Dan said.

Sam nodded back, just as officiously. "Dan."

"My sister here?" Dan asked, looking anything but pleased.

Her brother had to figure that she was, Sam thought, since Lulu's SUV was parked in his driveway. "Yes."

"Can I speak with her?"

Sam wasn't sure how to answer that. Generally, Lulu didn't want her family interfering in her personal business. And this definitely looked personal.

Before he could say anything further, Lulu strode across the living room and into the foyer. She regarded her brother with a mixture of annoyance and concern. "What's going on?" she asked.

Her older brother gave her a look that was strictly family-drama. He compressed his lips, looking over her pajamas. "I could ask you the same thing," he groused.

It didn't help, Sam thought, that with her flushed face and guilty eyes, it appeared as though Lulu had tumbled straight out of bed. *Sam's* bed.

She folded her arms, stubborn as ever. "I asked first."

Dan squinted at her. "I've been trying to get a hold of you since last evening."

"I was busy."

"Yeah, well, that's no reason not to answer your phone," he chastised.

"Actually," Lulu shot back, "it kind of is."

The siblings stared each other down.

Sam cleared his throat. He was all for gallantly coming to Lulu's aid, even if they were no longer a couple. On the other hand, he had no wish to insert himself into another family's drama. Plus, the boys, who were still busily building a block tower, didn't need to witness any quarreling. He cleared his throat and looked back at Lulu, who was still blocking the doorway. "If you'd like, I can step in so you can step out and talk in private," Sam offered mildly.

"Nope." Lulu lounged against the door frame, one ankle crossed over the other. She stared at Dan, nonchalant. "Whatever you have to say to me, big brother, can be said in front of Sam. And how did you know I was here, anyway?"

Dan shrugged. "Simple deduction. Sam was at your place yesterday, helping out and watching over you. Neither of you have been answering your phones. I figured something was going on."

Taken aback, Lulu paused. "That's no reason to spy on me."

"I wasn't spying," Dan continued quietly. "I just wanted to make sure you're safe."

Sam couldn't blame him for that.

And neither, as much as she wanted to, could Lulu. "Well," she said finally, "as you can see, I am."

"Uh-huh. It still doesn't explain why you're here now," Dan said.

"I would think that would be obvious." She pointed to Theo, Andrew and Ethan who were all still playing happily with their toys.

Dan turned to Sam. "So the word in town is true? You've just become legal guardian to three little ones?"

"Yes."

He turned back to his sister. "What do you have to do with this?"

She tensed. "I'm here, helping out."

Dan lifted a curious brow.

"By…um…nannying," she concluded reluctantly.

Her brother eyed her pajamas, which were quite chaste compared to some of the things Sam had once seen Lulu in. And would like to see again.

"Do Mom and Dad know you're now *working* for Sam?"

It felt more like working *with*, but whatever, Sam thought. It was clear they were going to have to renegotiate their deal, anyway.

Meanwhile, Lulu wasn't about to quibble over semantics. "What do you think?"

Dan squinted. "That you were probably afraid to tell them about any of this, never mind your sleeping over, for fear of what they'd say."

Lulu turned to Sam, clearly feeling that was out of line, even if Dan was family. "Would you deck him for me?"

"No." Although he wouldn't mind taking her in his arms again.

Her eyes lit up like firecrackers on the Fourth of July. "Why not?" she demanded, looking both confused and incensed. "You've never had trouble defending my honor before!"

True, Sam thought, but this was different. They weren't a couple now, although for parts of the previous night and this morning it almost felt as if they *could* be again. And because, as the primary caregiving adults in three vulnerable little boys' lives, they had to be adult about all this. She especially had to not care about what others thought, as long as the two of them knew what they were doing was right. "Because there are better ways to resolve conflict," he said wearily.

Lulu flushed again, for an entirely different reason this time, it seemed. Temper dissipating, she turned back to her brother, contrite. "Okay, sorry for overreacting."

He lifted a hand, understanding. "It's okay, sis. I know you have a lot going on."

Lulu regarded her brother intently. "Why did you want to talk to me, anyway?"

Dan relaxed as peace returned. "I wanted to tell you there was some news about your hives. The driver of the tractor trailer hauling the off-road forklifts was apprehended last night in Missouri."

Lulu bit her lip. "And the bees?"

"We don't know where they are yet. The two vehicles apparently split up. The guy who loaded the beehives into the refrigeration truck said he thought it was a legal transport."

Her shoulders slumped in disappointment. "What about all the honey that was stolen?"

"The jars are in crates, on the same truck as the beehives. He thought those were authorized to be removed, too."

Appearing distraught, Lulu moved closer to Sam. It was all he could do not to put his arm around her and hug her close. Figuring that was the last thing she would want him to do in front of her protective older brother, he remained where he was.

"Did the officers believe him?" she asked in a low, quavering voice.

Dan's brow furrowed. "Not sure, but the guy is cooperating, so there's a chance we might recover your bees yet."

"Thank heavens." Looking like she needed a moment to compose herself, Lulu went back into the ranch house without another word.

Dan declined to stay for breakfast. Intuiting Lulu's brother had a few more things he wanted to say, man-to-man, Sam walked him to his squad car.

"You and Lulu an item again?" Dan asked casually.

Sam shook his head. "No." *But after last night, I wish we were*, Sam thought. And how crazy was that?

The lawman slanted him a warning glance. "You know in addition to her usual impulsiveness, Lulu has baby fever…"

"She's also the next and last guardian on the list for the kids. She wants to be involved in this."

"You break her heart again," Dan warned, "friend of the family or not, you're going to be dealing with all five of her brothers. You get that?"

Sam nodded.

For a moment, neither of them spoke.

"So how is it going with the kids?" Dan asked.

Sam gave him the recap of the first eighteen hours.

Dan blinked, then offered empathetically, "I'm off at eleven. If you'd like, Kelly and I could round up our kids and come over this afternoon to lend a hand."

His wife was not only a preschool teacher, but mother to triplets, too. Sam spread his hands, for once open to any assistance offered. "Actually," he said sincerely, "if Kelly would like to visit, whatever tips she can give us would be great."

For the first time since he had arrived, Dan smiled. "I know she'd be glad to help," he said. "As would I."

Kelly, Dan and their triplets arrived shortly after noon, with a picnic lunch and a large box of toys their children had outgrown. Two-year-olds Theo, Andrew and Ethan were immediately taken with four-year-olds Michelle, Michael and Matthew.

Who had *lots* of questions.

"Are these your babies, Aunt Lulu?" Matthew asked.

"No." Looking gorgeous in a pair of coral shorts and a sleeveless white linen blouse, her hair swept up in a clip on the back of her head, Lulu knelt and lined up toy cars and trucks on the floor next to a play garage. Briefly, regret flashed in her long-lashed eyes. "I'm helping to take care of them," she explained, "but they're staying with Sam."

"So you're their daddy," Michael concluded with furrowed brow.

"Guardian," Sam corrected gently. *Although I'm beginning to think I'd like to be more than just that...*

Oblivious to the overemotional nature of his thoughts, Michelle sized up her aunt Lulu, then Sam. "Are you having a romance? 'Cause if you are," she added helpfully, "then you could get *married*."

Sam watched Lulu tense, the way she always did when the subject of her and marriage came up.

Kelly blushed. "Sorry." The lively preschool teacher lifted a hand. "She's been obsessed with love and weddings and marriage since..."

"Forever," Dan chuckled.

Michelle beamed. "Our mommy married Dan so he could be our daddy. They could show you how to fall in love. Then you could become a mommy like you want, Aunt Lulu," she finished sincerely.

So it was true, Sam thought. Dan hadn't been wrong in his analysis. And Lulu hadn't been exaggerating when she'd said she had wanted this forever. She did have baby fever. Enough to skew her judgment? Cause her to behave as recklessly as she had before they'd broken up? Only to regret her overly impulsive actions later? He sure as hell hoped not. Their first breakup had been excruciating enough. And now Theo, Andrew and Ethan were involved.

Seemingly aware of the delicate nature of the circumstances, Kelly took charge. "I think Sam and Aunt Lulu can figure out their own situation, honey."

"Let's show the boys the rest of the stuff we brought for them to play with," Dan said, digging into the big box of toys.

The kids immediately became enthralled, as everything old became new again.

Which was good, because it was only a few minutes later that the small moving van from Houston arrived.

"Where do y'all want this?" the workers asked. The crew boss opened up the back to reveal about twenty cardboard moving boxes, various toddler riding toys, a trio of toddler beds, a bureau, an oversize rocker-glider and a matching footstool.

Sam looked at Lulu, once again very glad she was there. "What do you think?" He had no idea where to put all this stuff.

"If it were me, I'd put the boxes containing Peter and Theresa's belongings in a storage area like…"

"The attic?"

"Yes. And then clear the large bedroom next to yours and set up a nursery for all three boys in there. Maybe figure out where to put the playroom stuff later."

Sam considered the suggestion. "Downstairs, off the kitchen, where my home office is now?"

"That would certainly be practical. You could toddler-proof the space and keep an eye on them while you prepare their meals. Maybe move your home office upstairs to one of the spare guest rooms you aren't really using. Where it'll be quieter."

Sam nodded gratefully. "Sounds good." He offered to pay the movers a little extra to lend a hand with the reorganization efforts. Two hours later, with Dan and Kelly still downstairs supervising both sets of triplets, he and Lulu remained upstairs, unpacking the nursery linens.

"You really don't have to help me with this," Lulu said. "Now that the beds are assembled and put in place, I can get it all set up from here. So, if you want to hook up the stuff in your new office space—" which was at the far end of the hall "—or go downstairs and work on the new playroom area…"

Why was she suddenly in such a hurry to get rid of him, now that the movers had left? Sam could only come up with one reason.

"Afraid what Kelly and Dan will think if you're alone with me for too long?"

"No." Her cheeks lit with embarrassment, she swooped down to pull pillows, mattress pads and sheets out of boxes.

Aware that everything but the possibility of making love to her again had temporarily left his brain, he lifted his brow. "Uh-huh." He watched her deposit the appropriate stack of linens on the end of each toddler bed with more than necessary care. "Then why didn't you tell anyone in your family that you were going to be the boys' nanny, at least temporarily?"

"Maybe I didn't have time."

He let their glances collide, then linger. "And maybe things haven't really changed since we were together before."

Looking adorably flustered, she whirled away from him and went back to the bed against the far wall. "I know what you thought back then. And apparently now, too," she said, her emotions suddenly as fired up as his. "But I was never ashamed to be with you."

"But you were reluctant to tell them just how serious we were about each other. Isn't that right, darlin'?" He paused to let his words sink in.

Her upright posture emphasized the soft swell of her breasts. His body hardened in response. "You may have been twenty-one," she mused, "but I had just turned nineteen…"

"Which was old enough to go to Tennessee with me for spring break."

"Yes, but my parents didn't know that." She bent to

put on the first mattress pad and gestured for him to do the same. "All they knew, or know even to this day, was that I was going to go with Theresa to visit Graceland and Dollywood and Gatlinburg, and then enjoy the music scene in Nashville…"

He tore his eyes from her sensational legs and the sweet curve of her hips, recalling, "They had no idea that you were going to be maid of honor and I was going to be best man at Peter and Theresa's elopement."

Cheeks turning pink, Lulu moved around to the other side of the bed to snap the elastic hem into place. "They wouldn't have approved."

He imagined they would have approved even less if they'd known she was deliberately keeping them in the dark. He finished putting the mattress cover on the second bed, then stood. "Are they going to approve of you nannying here?"

Lulu drew a deep breath. "If you want the truth…"

He did.

She put on the top sheet, then the quilt. "Probably not."

Finished, they both headed for the remaining toddler bed. Her head bent—to avoid his gaze, he imagined—she worked swiftly and methodically. He would have helped had she not edged him out with her hips.

Folding his arms, he moved around so he could see her expression. "You know you can't keep being here a secret from them, don't you?" Laramie County was a close-knit community, where families watched out for other families. Which meant that word would spread quickly.

Finished, Lulu punched the pillow into place. "I wasn't planning to."

"What's going to happen if they do express their displeasure?" he said, goading her. "Will just the *thought* of disappointing them make you run away again?"

She marched toward him, unafraid. "I never ran away." She poked a finger in his chest. "*You* were the one who threw down the gauntlet, *forcing* us to call it all off."

He went toe-to-toe with her and lowered his face until they were nose to nose. "For good reason, Lulu. I wasn't going to hide how I felt!"

"But you did," Lulu whispered, tears gleaming in her eyes. "We both did," she admitted in a choked voice, filled with the kind of heartache he, too, had experienced. "For a long time after that…"

Suddenly, Sam knew, he wasn't the only one who had been carrying a torch for the last ten years.

The next thing he knew, she was all the way in his arms. Her face turned up to his, and in that instant, all the pain of the last decade melted away. Their lips fused. A helpless sound escaped her throat and she pressed herself against him, yielding to him in a way she never had before.

And damn it if he wasn't giving his all to her, too. He gathered her even closer, let the kiss deepen, all the while savoring the sweet womanly taste of her, her fiery temperament, her warmth and her tenderness. Whether or not they'd be able to work it all out in the long haul was still questionable, but there'd never been anyone else for him. Never would be, he knew…

Lulu hadn't meant to let her feelings slip out. It wasn't surprising they had. She'd never been able to be around Sam and keep her guard up for long. He had a way of seeing past her defenses, of giving what was needed, even when she didn't exactly ask for it.

And what she needed right now, she thought as she

sank even deeper into his tantalizing embrace, was his strength and his tenderness, his kindness and perceptiveness. She needed to know if there was still something really special between them, or if their all-consuming feelings for each other had faded.

True, they hadn't made things work when they'd had a chance. And there was no way they could go back and undo any of those mistakes, much as she might wish.

They could, however, find a way to forge a new path, one that gave them both what they needed and wanted, she thought as his tongue swept her mouth and mated ever so evocatively with hers. What she wanted right now, she realized, pressing even closer, was a second chance.

For him. For her. Maybe even for the three kids that were legally in his charge and emotionally in hers.

Who knew what would have happened if not for the sounds of a delicately clearing throat? The sight of her sister-in-law in the doorway?

"Sorry to interrupt," Kelly said, her cheeks flushing. "But the kids are all getting hungry. Would you all be up for taking them into town for pizza?"

Chapter Six

"You really think this is going to work?" Sam asked Lulu at seven thirty that evening. He lounged against the bathroom wall, smelling like soap and man and brisk cologne. He also needed a shave. Although, truth be told, the rim of evening shadow on his jaw made him look rakishly sexy.

Trying not to think about how much she wanted to kiss him again, never mind how intimate and somehow right this all felt, Lulu squirted bubble bath soap into the big soaking tub in the master bathroom. As she turned on the warm water, she reflected how much better the triplets' second day at the ranch had gone, compared to the first. It gave her hope the boys might settle in after all. That with a little time and a lot of love and effort, she and Sam *could* handle this.

And if they could handle the boys' adjustment, what else might they be able to handle? she wondered. A real, enduring friendship? An affair? One thing was clear: the hot kiss they'd shared earlier was still resonating within her. And maybe him, too, if the veiled looks he'd been giving her were any indication.

With effort, she forced herself back to the matter at hand. "You heard what Kelly said at dinner. A familiar routine is crucial in helping kids to feel safe and happy."

He cocked a brow, his gaze drifting over her lazily. In the same casual tone, he returned, "And the second thing is making kids *want* to do what they need to do."

"Right." Lulu smiled. Hence, the stop at the discount superstore on the way out of town to let Ethan, Andrew and Theo all pick out new bath toys. The boys had ridden back to the ranch with their treasures clutched in their little arms. And now that Sam had removed the packaging for them, it was time to play.

He walked back into the bedroom, where the triplets were enthusiastically climbing up onto the storage bench at the foot of his bed, and from there, onto the mattress. "Who wants to put their toys in the bubbles?" he asked.

"Me do!" Andrew said, hopping over to the edge and leaping unexpectedly into Sam's arms.

"Me first!" Theo dropped down and scooted over to the edge of the bed, putting his feet over the side of the mattress and onto the wooden bench, then down onto the floor.

Ethan held out his arms joyously and waited to be scooped up. "Me, too!"

"Okay, fellas," Sam said, once they'd all been ushered into the bathroom. "Let's see which new toys like the bath the most."

Andrew dropped his rubber whale and dolphins in. The creatures shimmied but remained upright. Theo added his waterwheel, sieve and cup. Ethan added his three boats. Sam nodded approvingly at them. "Looking good," he said.

"Play?" Theo asked. He already had one leg up.

"Sure," Lulu said matter-of-factly, "but you have to take your dirty clothes off first, before you get in."

Immediately, all three boys began to undress. Lulu and Sam helped. A minute later, they were all in the tub, playing merrily. And were so entranced by their toys, they endured quick shampoos and rinses, too.

Eventually, they had to get out.

They did not want to do that.

Lulu said, "We have cookies and milk and bedtime stories for three little boys, as soon as they get their jammies on."

They had to think about it. But eventually caved. And by eight thirty, the five of them were on Sam's sofa again, enjoying what was to become their new bedtime routine. She and Sam alternated the reading of the stories, while the boys snuggled close, and cozy contentment flowed through them all.

Once again, the boys fell asleep sprawled together like a pile of puppies on the center of the sofa. Sam looked over at her. The tender regard he bestowed on the boys seemed to include her, too.

A shiver of awareness went through her.

"Move them now, or wait?" he inquired huskily.

It was a toss-up either way. Lulu studied their cherubic faces, then said, "Let's give them a few minutes." Aware her heartbeat had accelerated for no reason she could figure, she gathered up the basket of the boys' laundry that she'd left at the foot of the staircase. "Okay if I use your machine?"

Sam eased away from the sleeping trio, while Beauty dozed nearby, watching over the triplets. "Sure. I'll help."

They went into the laundry room together. Began sorting. Light colors in one pile, darks in another. They added their clothes, too.

He stepped back while she put in the first load, added detergent, switched on the machine. In the small space, it was impossible not to notice the silky smooth skin of her legs beneath the hem of her shorts. He lifted his gaze, taking in the curve of her hips, her slender waist and full breasts, before returning to her face. "It was a much better day," he remarked, aware he hadn't felt this relaxed and happy in a long time.

She smiled back at him. "It was."

As she started to move past him, he captured her in his arms. "On all scores," he rasped, then lowered his head and kissed her tenderly.

She caught her breath, even as she softened against him. Splaying her hands across his hard chest, she submitted to another kiss and then surprised him with a passionate one of her own. "Are we really doing this?" Lulu whispered. "Flirting with romance again?"

They'd be doing more than just flirting if he had his way. Knowing, though, if they were to have any chance at success, they'd have to slow down a bit, Sam gave her waist a playful squeeze. "We really are," he said.

Knowing they could have a rough night ahead, they both turned in shortly after that. Ten hours later, Sam woke slowly, feeling an incredible sense of well-being, a weight on his chest and each shoulder, and the soft press of a female body draped against his right flank. The fragrant scent of citrus and flowers teasing his nostrils, he turned his head slightly as he opened his eyes. Caught a glimpse of Lulu's lustrous hair as the top of her head pressed against his cheek. She shifted slightly, sighing drowsily. Snuggled deeper into the crook of his shoulder. She had a little boy in her arms, too.

In a rush of memory, it all came flooding back to him.

They'd had another night of the kids waking after a few hours with night terrors, crying incessantly, refusing to be soothed. He and Lulu had paced the floor in tandem, toddlers in their arms. Until finally, exhausted, they all climbed into his big bed, and still holding on to each other, slipped one by one into an exhausted sleep.

Made easier by one thing, the fact they were all in this together.

Lulu sighed again and opened her eyes all the way. She appeared to struggle to orient herself, just as he had, then relaxed as the events of the night came flooding back. She turned to gaze into his eyes. "Morning," she mouthed, as if leery of waking the little guy draped across her chest.

"Morning to you," he mouthed back with a grin. There was at least one perk to another stressful, sleepless night. He had forgotten what it had been like to wake up with her beside him. Not that he'd enjoyed it too many times before Tennessee. But the week they'd spent together prior to their breakup, that had been something special.

And now, thanks to the arrival of the triplets, he and Lulu were back to spending lots of time together again.

Without warning, three little heads popped up, one by one. The boys studied Lulu and Sam. Grinned at each other and scrambled upright. "Hungry," Ethan announced.

"Want 'cakes," Andrew said.

Meaning pancakes, Sam thought, recalling how more had been squished between little fingers and smeared across plates than eaten the previous day.

"No. Eggs," Theo declared.

"No, cereal!" Ethan disagreed.

"How about all three?" Lulu said.

Sam grinned. "Given how hungry I am, sounds good to me."

They worked together, cooking and supervising. Of course it was a lot easier, now that they'd moved the boys' toys to the adjacent family room.

"Well, that went better," Sam said half an hour later.

"It did, didn't it?" Lulu replied, pleased.

She looked gorgeous, lounging around his kitchen. He tore his gaze from the flattering fit of her pajamas and moved it to her tousled, honey-brown hair and pink cheeks. "So well," he added expansively, "that if you'd like time off to go to the McCabe family potluck at your brother Jack's house this afternoon, I think it would be okay."

Lulu's brow rose. "You know about that?"

Sam sipped his second mug of coffee. "Dan mentioned it last night at dinner, when he and I went up to the counter to collect our pizzas. He said we would all be welcome, of course, but that if the kids and I were to go with you, there might be…" He paused, unsure how to word it.

"Flack from my parents?" Lulu guessed. She reached for a bottle of spray cleaner and began wiping down the counters for the second time.

Sam concentrated on the smooth, purposeful movements of her hands. His mouth suddenly dry, he shrugged. "Anyway, I know that they both think I'm a fine enough person, apart from you."

Lulu dropped the used paper towel into the trash. Straightened. "They haven't exactly been your cheerleader, when it comes to me, anyway. Not since we broke up years ago," she concluded.

That was putting it lightly, Sam thought. Maybe it was time they talked about this. "I think they blame me—

and the animosity of our breakup—for the fact you've never married anyone else and have yet to get the family of your own that you want." He knew the same could probably be said of him.

"And they're probably right." Lulu raked the edge of her teeth across the soft curve of her lower lip. "You are the reason I've never been serious about anyone else."

She hadn't meant to blurt that out. But now that she had…maybe, given the fact they were trying to get their relationship back on an amiable track…it was time the two of them were more forthright with each other than they had been. She closed the distance between them and slid her hands into his.

"No one has ever compared, in terms of the way you made me feel back then," she confessed. Aware the past tense wasn't entirely accurate, given the whirl her emotions were in.

"Same here," he said gruffly, the expression on his face maddeningly inscrutable.

"But that doesn't mean marriage isn't in both our futures. Someday," she continued hopefully. Even though the only person she could imagine tying the knot with was Sam.

An awkward silence fell.

Lulu reluctantly disengaged their palms and stepped away.

"Back to the potluck at Jack's today," Sam said finally.

She walked over to look out the window. Although rain was predicted for that evening, it was bright and sunny now. "I want you and the boys to go with me."

"Sure?" His gaze roved over her.

Lulu turned back to face him, certain about this much.

"If I'm going to be your nanny, my family needs to get used to seeing us together."

The rest of the morning was spent supervising the kids, finishing the laundry they'd started the evening before and showering. They also dealt with their personal responsibilities.

Sam talked to his foreman about the work being done on his ranch.

Lulu called a couple of her beekeeping friends, explaining that in addition to the theft, she was now busy helping out a friend who was weathering a family crisis. She arranged for them to install a new queen and help her tend her remaining hive for the next two weeks.

And of course, they all had to get dressed for the potluck.

By the time they had everyone ready to go, it was nearly one in the afternoon, and the kids, who were sleep deprived, were getting cranky and yawning. Beauty, looking ready for peace and quiet, climbed onto her cushion in the corner of the kitchen.

Sam's hand lightly touched Lulu's waist as they moved through the doorway, then just as easily fell away.

Yet the moment of casual gallantry stayed with her a lot longer than it should have.

Doing her best to disguise the shiver of awareness sifting through her, she guided the boys into the back seat of Sam's extended cab pickup. He went around to the other side and leaned in to help fasten the safety harnesses. "Think they'll sleep on the way into town?" he asked.

Lulu climbed into the pickup, too, then handed the boys the bucket hats and sunglasses they wore in the car. "I hope they can power nap." She smiled as they put them on, then glanced over at Sam, looking across the row of three car seats. "Or will at least behave long enough for me to dash into the market and pick up the loaves of bread I was requested to bring."

Five minutes later, Sam said, "Luck is with us."

Lulu followed his glance.

All three boys had nodded off. Blankets and stuffed animals clutched to their chests. Lulu sighed, the affection she felt for them nearly overwhelming her. "They look so sweet right now," she whispered, stunned by the ferocity of her feelings. She turned back to Sam and, unable to stop herself, asked, "Is it weird for me to be so attached to them already?"

He shook his head. "They need us." His sensual lips took on a pensive curve as his hands tightened on the steering wheel. "And I'm beginning to think we need them, too."

His husky observation sent a thrill down her spine. She shifted in her seat to better view his ruggedly handsome profile. "How so?"

"To rekindle our friendship, for one thing."

He was so matter-of-fact, so certain. Her heart skittering in her chest, Lulu drew in a whiff of his tantalizing aftershave. "Do you think this is all part of some big predestined plan for our lives?" That everything they'd experienced up to now had led them to this day?

A muscle ticked in his jaw. He seemed so serious now, in the way that said he wanted the two of them to get closer. The hell of it was, she wanted that, too. "How else to explain it?" he asked.

How else indeed, Lulu wondered, if not fate?

When they stopped at a traffic light at the edge of town, he turned to her. His gaze swept over her, lingering briefly on her lips, before returning to her eyes. "Neither of us had seen Peter or Theresa for years, yet they both put us on the potential guardian list. Everyone else ahead of us failed. And the triplets end up here in Laramie County with us."

What was that, if not some sort of sign? Lulu did her best to keep from overreacting. "According to the will, they were just supposed to be with you, though," she pointed out softly.

He looked deep into her eyes, his gratitude apparent. "But, darlin', you knew without even seeing them that they were going to need both of us. And you stepped in, initially over my reservations. And now—" he reached over to briefly squeeze her hand "—barely three days later, we're together twenty-four-seven and feeling like our own little family unit."

For now, Lulu thought worriedly.

What if they got to the point where he didn't need her at night? Or left the boys with her, by herself, all day? As they had originally planned?

As much as the hopeless romantic in her wanted to wish otherwise, she had to remember that she was still involved only because he was allowing it. She had no legal standing here. So, if they were to start not getting along again...or decide there was no rekindled romance for them in the cards...their situation could change in a heartbeat.

The light turned green and Sam drove on.

"Um...speaking of destiny..." Lulu drew in a shaky breath.

Sam quirked a brow, listening.

"As heartbreaking...and yet simultaneously incredible...as this has all been for us," she began, knitting her hands together in her lap, "I still feel it's an awfully fragile situation."

Sam turned into the supermarket parking lot. He parked in a space and left the motor running. The boys slept on. One hand resting on the steering wheel, he turned and took in the anguished expression on her face. "Something on your mind?" he asked.

Lulu nodded, her heart in her throat. She didn't want to do this but she knew it had to be said. Sooner, rather than later.

Still holding Sam's eyes, she vowed softly, "I just want you to know that whatever happens…" *between you and me and the rest of it* "…I'm never going to emotionally abandon those boys."

Not exactly a ringing endorsement of their future, Sam thought, stunned by the sudden doubt she was harboring about this situation working out as they hoped.

He was about to ask what had caused her to be so on edge. But before he could speak, she slipped out of the truck, eased the passenger door shut and headed for the supermarket entrance.

As Sam had feared, the lack of forward motion had an effect.

By the time she returned a few minutes later with four bakery-fresh loaves of bread and a basket of fresh Texas peaches in hand, the boys were all awake and kicking their legs rambunctiously. Lulu seemed just as impatient. "On to Jack's!" she said.

Although Sam knew all the McCabes and their loved ones, he had never spent a lot of time in their company. The year he and Lulu had been dating, she had preferred to keep their relationship separate from her family obligations.

And while part of him had felt a little excluded back then, the rest of him had been happy to have Lulu all to himself. So it felt a little different now to be walking in with her and the boys when the rest of her family, sans her parents, was already there in Jack's big shady backyard.

Together, they made the rounds, saying hello to everyone. Her brother Matt was there with the love of his life, Sara Anderson, and her nine-month-old son, Charley. Matt looked happier than Sam had ever imagined he could be again when he'd first returned from war.

Cullen and his newly pregnant wife, Bridgett, introduced their adopted eighteen-month-old son, Robby, to the boys, who were immediately taken with him.

Jack's three daughters, Chloe, Nicole and Lindsay, ages three, four and six, also came over to say hi.

Lulu's brother Chase and his wife, Mitzy, introduced their ten-month-old quadruplet sons.

And of course the triplets were already acquainted with Dan and Kelly's four-year-olds—Matthew, Michael and Michelle.

In no time, the fifteen kids were scattered on the blankets spread across the lawn, playing with the toys that had been set out. Jack had the grill going, and all the other adults were gathered around, talking in small groups.

And Lulu, it seemed, couldn't wait to get away from him, Sam noted, as she touched his arm, her manner pleasant but oddly aloof. Like he was just another random guest in attendance at the barbecue. Not her old friend, not her potential love interest and certainly not her date for the occasion.

"Can I get you anything?" she asked, an officious smile pasted on her face. "A cold drink, maybe?"

He thought of the afternoon ahead. The fact he was suddenly and unexpectedly being pushed out of Lulu's life, just as he had been before.

Aware they had an audience, he smiled back at her in the exact same way. "Sounds great. Thanks."

* * *

Lulu made her escape, just as her parents' Escalade pulled up in front of Jack's home. She didn't know what to expect from them when they finally talked. She just knew she was dreading it.

"So what do you ladies have planned for Father's Day?" Kelly was asking when Lulu walked into Jack's kitchen to see what she could do to help.

"Don't know yet." Bridgett sighed.

"Me, either, although the kids and I still have a few days to figure it out," Kelly said.

"Should one of us ask Jack's girls what they'd like to do for him?" Lulu's mother, Rachel, asked as she came in, carrying a large platter of veggies and ranch dip.

Bess Monroe, Jack's friend—and constant platonic companion—smiled shyly and said, "I could probably do that if y'all would like." Although technically not family to anyone here besides her twin, Bridgett, Bess was around enough to be unofficially considered so.

Lulu smiled. "I think that would be great."

Rachel set the platter down, then turned back to Lulu, wasting no time at all in doing what Lulu had feared she might. "Sweetheart," she said softly, "could we have a word?"

"Sure." Lulu followed her mother into Jack's formal living room at the front of the big Victorian. Her dad was waiting there.

"What's this we hear about you becoming a *nanny* for the three kids Sam is guardian to?" Frank asked, his brow furrowed in concern.

Briefly, Lulu explained the situation while her parents listened.

"I understand he's probably got his hands full, but do

you really think you should be this involved?" Rachel asked kindly.

Yes, Lulu thought. "I'm next on the list of potential guardians, Mom."

To Lulu's relief, her parents weren't as disappointed in her as she had feared they might be.

"*Next* being the operative word," her father pointed out gently.

"We just don't want to see you get too attached, sweetheart," Rachel said, "since the boys really are Sam's charges."

Frowning worriedly, her dad added, "And the two of you have a history of not getting along…"

That they did, Lulu admitted reluctantly to herself. But all that had changed. The last three days were proof of that. She and Sam had been not only getting along splendidly, but working like a well-rehearsed team. "That was because we were broken up," Lulu explained practically.

Her mother did a double take. "Are you saying you're *not* broken up any more?"

Lulu flushed, not sure how to respond.

Rachel lifted both hands, pleading, "Oh, Lulu." She came forward swiftly to embrace her. "Please don't do anything reckless that you'll regret later!"

"I don't intend to, Mom," Lulu said, returning her mother's hug.

"Good," her dad said in relief. He embraced her, too. Stepped back. "Because the last thing we want to see is you heartbroken the way you were before."

Lulu shoved aside the memories of that awful time. "I'm not going to be." She looked both her parents in the eye.

Her mom paused. "How can you be sure of that?"

Easy, Lulu thought. "Because Sam and I are not the

naive kids we were ten years ago. We've grown and matured," she insisted, doing her best to reassure her parents. "There is no way we're making the same mistakes."

Different ones, maybe.

But even those they should be equipped to handle, she promised herself resolutely.

Rachel exhaled. "So you *are* back together?" she pressed.

Knowing a few stolen kisses did not constitute a reconciliation, Lulu shook her head. "No, Mom, we're not." The hell of it was, she just wished they were. And she wasn't sure how any of them, her parents or herself, should feel about that.

Chapter Seven

"Are you avoiding me?" Sam asked an hour later, when he finally caught up with Lulu in the walk-in pantry off the kitchen.

Actually, yes, I am.

Determined not to give her parents anything to discuss later, she looked behind him, saw no one in their line of sight and slid him a glance. If only he weren't six feet three inches of masculine perfection, didn't know her inside and out and didn't kiss like a dream, this would be a whole lot easier.

Lulu continued counting out paper plates and putting them in the wicker basket at her hip. Wishing he didn't look so big and strong and immovable standing next to her, she asked, "Why would you think that?"

"Oh, I don't know." His lazy quip brought heat to her cheeks. "Maybe the fact that you've managed to stay as far away from me as possible since your parents got here this afternoon."

Aware he was watching her, gauging her reactions as carefully as she was measuring his, Lulu lifted her chin. "It's just…there's a lot to do," she fibbed, "if we're going to get this meal on before the rain starts…" Hoping to distract him, she asked, "By the way, who's watching the boys?"

"Your mom and dad."

Lulu winced. Of all the people to tell he was going in search of her.

"Why? Is there something wrong with that?" Sam asked. Clad in a blue short-sleeved button-down, jeans and boots, he looked sexy and totally at ease. "They offered, and they've obviously got plenty of experience handling little ones."

"I know."

"Then?" he asked. His gaze roved her knee-length white shorts and sleeveless Mediterranean-blue blouse before returning to her face.

"It's just…the boys can be a lot."

They both stopped as the sound of…was that rain…?

"Oh no!" Lulu exclaimed, pushing past Sam, seeing through the kitchen windows that a sudden downpour had indeed begun. "Everyone's still outside!"

They took off at a run.

Theo was in the sandbox, trying to protect his creation from the torrential downpour to no avail. He was screaming in distress, along with two of Jack's daughters who also did not want to see their castles destroyed. Neither were listening to Lulu's mom, who was trying to coax them inside.

Andrew was standing on the top of the play-fort slide, along with three-year-old Chloe, enjoying the downpour and also refusing to get down for Bess Monroe—who might have been able to handle one child but definitely could not pick up two simultaneously.

Ethan, wide-eyed with a mixture of surprise and dismay, had taken cover beneath an umbrella table and was also refusing to be coaxed out by Lulu's dad.

Plus, the food on the long picnic tables needed to be rescued. Luckily, it was covered with plastic wrap, but still...

"You get Ethan, I'll get the other two," Sam said.

Every adult jumped in to help.

A frantic five minutes later, their meal had been salvaged, and everyone was inside. And while Jack's Victorian was pretty spacious, the fourteen adults and fifteen children had the first floor bursting at the seams. So, as soon as the meal was over, cleanup done, the great exodus began.

Not surprisingly, the triplets were having so much fun playing with the other kids, they did not want to leave.

"Five more minutes," Lulu said firmly.

"And then we're going back to the ranch to see Beauty," Sam added.

The mention of the beloved pet had all three boys hesitating but not for long.

"No! Stay!" Andrew shouted cantankerously.

"Play! More!" Theo added while Ethan pretended to ignore it all and kept right on driving his toy trucks around in circles.

Sam and Lulu exchanged the kind of looks parents had exchanged forever. A fact that, unfortunately, did not go unnoticed by Lulu's mother.

"One way or another..." Sam murmured.

Lulu nodded. "I agree." The kids had to have boundaries. And when they were overtired, their belligerence only got worse. So even if it meant they were unhappy, they were still going to have to leave when the time was up.

Sam moved off to talk to Dan, to see if there had been any update on Lulu's bees. There had not.

Meanwhile, Kelly noted sympathetically, "The boys really seem to enjoy playing with other children. Did they go to preschool previously? Do you know?"

"From what Sam and I have been able to glean from their records," Lulu said, "Theresa went back to work part-time when the triplets were a year old. They went to school five mornings a week, from nine to one, for about six months, then bumped it up to six hours a day. They usually got picked up right after nap time."

"You could enroll them at the preschool where I teach. Especially if you think that would help them acclimate."

Lulu hesitated.

Kelly continued, "Cece has the two-year-old class, and she's great with them."

Reluctantly, Lulu admitted, "Well, Sam is the one who has the say on that, but I don't know that he'll want to leave them. Especially since they've been moved around so much already in the last two months."

Kelly smiled. "I understand. If you change your mind, let me know because I can really expedite the process for you all."

"Thanks, Kelly."

Sam approached. "Ready to give it another try?"

Feeling as much a mommy as he appeared to be a daddy, Lulu nodded.

They tried reason, cajoling and firmly ordering. No approach worked when it came to getting their way-too-overtired children to cooperate. In the end, they had no choice but to carry all three boys out to Sam's pickup in the still pouring rain. Jack loaned them some beach towels to throw over their heads to keep the boys from getting wet, but Sam and Lulu both got rained on nevertheless.

Sam seemed impervious to the chill. Lulu was not

so lucky. Shivering, she draped one of the damp towels across her shoulders and chest, like a shawl, the other over her bare legs as they drove away.

By the time they reached the first stoplight in the downtown area of Laramie, the boys had stopped their protesting and were already yawning. They were sound asleep at the town limits.

Lulu told Sam what Kelly had said about enrolling them in preschool.

"Hmm."

"What does hmm mean?"

He slanted her a self-effacing smile. "It means, like you, I'm on the fence. I think it would be good for their social development, but I worry that more change might make things worse."

Lulu blew out a breath. Not really all that surprised to find them feeling the exact same thing. "Being a parent is hard."

He reached over and squeezed her knee through the towel. "We'll get used to it," he promised.

We'll...

He had said *we'll*.

They really were in this together, Lulu thought.

It was still raining pretty hard fifteen minutes later when they arrived back at the ranch. Sam parked as close as he could to the covered front porch, and they carried the boys in one at a time, with Sam easing the sleeping children from their car seats and Lulu holding a towel over them to keep them dry. They put them all on the sofa, placed their stuffed animals in their arms and covered them with their baby blankets.

Beauty strolled in to say hi. After she'd been let out for a quick potty break, she sank down next to the boys and curled up with her back to the sofa to nap while guarding her little charges.

Arms folded, Sam stood back to look at them. Tenderness sweeping through him, he leaned down to whisper in Lulu's ear, "Boy, they are really out."

"I know," she whispered back fondly.

And it was way too late for them to be taking a long nap. He glanced at his watch. "It's five o'clock."

She wrinkled her nose in concern, a sentiment he shared.

Hand beneath her elbow, he steered her a distance away. "Think we should wake them up? Or let them snooze a little while longer?"

She sent another affectionate look at the boys. As she swung back to him, he couldn't help but admire the sheen of her honey-brown hair. "I don't know." Lulu bit down on her lower lip, and heat pooled through him as she came intimately close. "What do you think?"

As if he were the expert here.

Still, it felt good to be sharing responsibility with her. To be able to lean on each other, whenever, however, they needed. Had they been able to do that before, they probably never would have broken up.

"Maybe a little while longer?" Sam supposed, inhaling her intoxicating perfume. "Until six?"

Their gazes met and she drew a breath. "Then we can let them play a bit before dinner, give them baths and go through the normal bedtime routine?"

"Sounds good," he said, his gaze dropping to her mouth, then lower, to the damp clothing clinging to her supple curves.

"What isn't good," Lulu said, holding her shirt out away from her breasts before allowing it to fall into place again, "is how I feel."

His body hardening at the sight of her nipples showing through her drenched shirt, he looked down at his own clothes. "We did get a little wet, didn't we, darlin'?"

Lulu grimaced. "I need to change. Unfortunately, I'm out of clean clothes, and I'm reluctant to leave you alone with the boys to make the run back to the Honeybee Ranch."

Not wanting her to go, either, Sam shrugged. "You can borrow one of my shirts." The way she had when they'd spent their spring break in Tennessee. When their attraction to each other was white-hot. Life was so much simpler back then.

Her brow pleated. She didn't appear to be affected with the same memories. "You wouldn't mind?"

"Nah. Besides..." he let his glance sift over the damp, mussed strands of her sun-kissed honey-brown hair "... there's no point in going home to get more clothes when you can throw your laundry in my machines, get it washed and dried in an hour and a half or so. Probably be easier than running back and forth."

"Okay. Thanks." She squared her shoulders and took another deep breath. "You want to get me a shirt, then?"

Sam studied the color that had swept into her fair cheeks. He shrugged. "Just go to my closet and take any one you want. They're all on hangers."

Her flush deepened. "I think I'd feel better about it if you went with me."

Grinning, he gestured broadly. And tried not to think about how much he wanted to make love to her again. "If the lady insists..."

She led the way, with Sam behind her, admiring her every languid, graceful step. When they reached the bedroom doorway, she hesitated. He walked ahead to throw open the closet door, then stepped back. "Take your pick."

Bypassing the nicer ones at the front, she selected a worn blue chambray at the very back. Holding it in front of her, she pivoted back to face him. "This one okay?"

He nodded. "Perfect," he said huskily.

She read his mind, as their eyes met. "Oh, Sam…" she said, her hushed voice sliding like silk over his skin. The shirt she was holding fell to the floor. She stepped into his arms, rose on tiptoe and pressed her lips against his. Her kiss was everything he wanted. Tender. Searching. Sweetly tempting. A rush of molten desire swept through him. This was what he needed. *She* was what he needed. And damn it, he thought as her soft, pliant body surrendered all the more, if she didn't realize it, too.

Kissing Sam again was going to be a risk, Lulu knew. And she had avoided risks like the plague since the two of them had broken up. But the last few days had ignited a fire in her unlike anything she had ever felt, then or now. For good reason, it seemed. Sam was right to think this was all part of some larger destiny that brought them back into each other's lives, just in time to be able to help the boys and resurrect a replacement for the complete family they'd lost.

They were meant to be.

And what better way to prove it than through renewed lovemaking?

Giving in to the passion simmering between them, she dared him to take full advantage of fate and be as impulsive as she was. When he kissed her back with equal fervor, elation flowed through her. Caught up in the moment, she poured everything she had into their embrace. Her knees weakened, her whole body shivered. She hadn't ever felt this much like a woman, or wanted Sam with such unbridled passion. But she wanted him now, wanted him to fill up the aching loneliness deep inside her. She wanted him to help her live her life fully again.

And still he kissed her, hard and wet and deep. Masterfully taking charge, until she shifted restlessly against him, wanting more. His hands slid beneath her blouse to unfasten her bra and caress her erect nipples. His lips parted hers, his tongue sweeping into her mouth, until her entire body was on fire. She moaned at the delicious pressure, the taste and feel of him. Yanked her blouse over her head, let her bra fall to the floor.

His eyes darkened. "So beautiful," he said, his thumbs gently tracing the curves of her breasts, caressing her sensitive nipples. "More so…" he bent to lay a trail of kisses over her throat, collarbone, the tips of her breasts "…than I remember…"

Lord, he was gorgeous, too. All over. She tugged off his shirt, ran her hands over his chest. Explored the satiny warmth of his lean waist, muscled torso and broad shoulders. It had been so long since they'd made love. Too long, she mused as she ran her fingers through the crisp hair arrowing down into the waistband of his jeans.

Quivering with excitement, she slid her hands beneath. Cupped the hot, velvety hardness. He dropped his head, kissing her again, bringing forth another wellspring of desire. Their tongues tangled as surely as their hearts, and he groaned, resting his forehead on hers. "Lulu…" he whispered, the last of his gallantry fading fast.

She knew how easy it would be to fall in love with him all over again. Knew it and welcomed it. "I know what I'm doing, Sam," she whispered. She went to shut the bedroom door, then took him by the hand and led him toward the bed.

"Do you?" Eyes dark, he watched her continue to undress.

She knew what he was thinking; there had been so much hurt between them in the past. Too much. But that was over. It was a new day. One that held the promise of so much more.

There would not be regrets this time, she told herself fiercely. Even if they'd been brought together again by circumstances not of their own making, and were moving a little too fast.

"I know this feels reckless," she whispered. Her heart skittering in anticipation of the mind-blowing passion to come, she helped him disrobe, too. "But I want you. I've never stopped wanting you," she confessed with a ragged sigh.

Shouldn't that be enough?

Now that they were both adults with another full decade of life experience informing them?

With long-established ways to guard their hearts?

Suddenly, she wasn't the only one shuddering with pent-up need. "Well, in that case…" His sexy grin widened. All too ready to oblige, he dropped a string of kisses down her neck, across the slopes of her breasts to the crests, then he sank to his knees and his lips moved lower still. The white-hot intimacy had her arching in pleasure. Making her feel ravished and cherished all at once.

Closing her eyes, she fisted her hands in his hair and gave herself over to him. Fully. Completely. And she lost what little was left of her restraint as a soft moan and a shudder of overwhelming heat swept through her.

Hands on his shoulders, she urged him upward. Not about to be the only one to find release, she whispered against his shoulder, "My turn now."

Sam laughed quietly, as she'd hoped he would.

Determined to keep it light and sexy between them,

she was eager to tantalize his hot, hard body as he had hers. She lay down beside him, kissing and caressing him until everything fell away but the feel and touch and taste of him. Until there was no more holding back.

He found a condom. Together, they rolled it on. Suddenly, she was on her back. One hand was beneath her, lifting her, the other was between her thighs. She surged against him, softness to hardness. He stroked his thumb over her flesh, and she was flying, gone. And still he kissed her, again and again, until there wasn't any place she would rather be.

Needing him to find the same powerful release, Lulu wrapped her arms around him and brought him closer. He groaned, rough and low in his throat, and her muscles tautened as he found his way home in one long, slow, purposeful slide. Allowing her to adjust to the weight and size of him, he went deeper still.

Needing more, she wrapped her legs around his waist, opening up to him, and then there was nothing but the sensation of being taken, possessed. Treasured. And for the first time in an extremely long time, she felt connected to him in that very special man-woman way.

Sam had known it was a mistake to make love to Lulu on a whim. Because it was when Lulu did things on impulse that she was most likely to regret them later. But when she'd reached out to him, he hadn't been able to resist. Now, he was beginning to wish he had, as he watched Lulu silently come to the same conclusion that he had already reached. That once again, they'd let their emotions get the best of them, and had gone too far, too fast. "Us being together this way doesn't have to complicate things unnecessarily," he said, stroking a hand through her hair and soothing her as best he could. "We can still take things one day, one moment at a time, dar-lin'. Do whatever feels right."

Like make love.

And get closer yet.

"You're right." Lulu let out a long sigh. Pressed her hand against the center of his chest, insinuating distance between them. As their gazes locked, something came and went in her pretty eyes. "This doesn't have to mean anything more than any other fling would."

He held tight when she would have fled, aware once again she was taking his intentions all wrong. "That's not what I said," he told her gruffly.

"Isn't it?" she returned with a casual smile that did not reach her eyes. Before he could say anything else, she lifted a hand. "It's okay, Sam." With typical grace, she eased away from him. "We're both sophisticated enough to handle just having sex."

Which was obviously all it had been to her.

"And you're right," she finished with a weariness that seemed to come straight from her soul. "It really doesn't have to change anything." She rose and pulled on her panties and his shirt, then, scooping up her damp clothes, padded down the hall to the guest room where she'd been stowing her belongings.

He rose and dressed, too, in dry clothing. Emerging from his bedroom, he caught sight of her as she headed downstairs, small mesh bag of dirty clothes in hand.

Sam went back to gather up his own laundry, then found her in the utility room, sorting clothes, her head averted. He noted she had added an above-the-knee denim skirt and pretty sandals to her ensemble.

"Are we really just going to leave it like this?" he said, dumping his own clothing into a separate hamper.

Cheeks slightly pink, she kept her attention on her

task. "What's there to say?" They both reached for the detergent at the same time. Their shoulders and arms brushed before they could draw back.

Wishing he could make love to her again—without driving her further away than she was at this moment—he stepped back to give her the physical space she craved. He focused on the tumult in her eyes.

"Maybe you should tell me."

She looked at him for a long moment. "Well, it was probably important for us to satisfy our curiosity, given the situation."

She focused on her task, added soap, set the dials and closed the lid. Turned on the machine.

He stayed his ground. "Curiosity," he repeated. *So that's what they were calling it now.*

"We probably also needed to find out if the sparks we used to have still existed." She drew in a deep breath and finally pivoted to meet his gaze. Her chin lifted. "And now we know."

Now they did know. Though he had the intuition that they had arrived at completely different conclusions...

"Meaning what?"

She walked past him, down the hall, peered around the corner into the living room. The triplets were all still fast asleep. She returned to the kitchen, still not clarifying what she meant.

Knowing nothing would ever be solved by pretending there wasn't a problem, he edged closer. Needing to know where he stood with her. Guessed, "Meaning...it's not going to happen again?" Or it would?

She leaned against the kitchen island, her back to the still-pouring rain, and let out a slow breath. "I'm not sure."

He switched on the overhead lights, bringing light to the gloomy room. He moved so she had no choice but to look at him. "Hey," he said softly, not about to let her deny it. His gaze roved her. "I know it was good for you."

She blushed at his needling tone. "I know it was good for you, too." Seeing Beauty heading for the back door, she moved to open it. Stepped out under the overhang. "But as you noted earlier, our life is pretty complicated right now, with the kids and all," she said, keeping her voice low as the damp warmth surrounded them.

Sam gave his pet room to move down the steps, into the yard, then eased next to Lulu. "And making love just now makes it even more so. I get that. It doesn't mean we can pretend it didn't happen," he pointed out. Or that he even wanted to.

Regret pinched the corners of her mouth. "Sure about that?"

Because she sure seemed able to do so, Sam noted bitterly as Beauty came back up the deck steps and walked on into the house.

Lulu grabbed a dog towel off the hook and bent to dry off Beauty's thick coat. When she was done, she gave the Saint Bernard a fond pat on the head and watched as the dog padded soundlessly back to the living room, to stand guard once again over the kids.

Lulu hung up the towel, then, glancing over at the family room, zeroed in on the toys that had been left all over the place. She breezed past him and began picking them up. Although he didn't care whether the toys were neatly put away or not, he followed and began to help.

An even more conflicted silence fell. Which was a shame, Sam thought, since they didn't often have time to themselves. "You really don't want to talk about this any more?" he said, wishing like hell that she would.

Still bearing the glow of their lovemaking, she bit her

lip. Ambivalence flooded her expression. "I really don't," she returned, just as softly.

And suddenly, Sam knew what the real problem likely was.

"Then how about you tell me what happened at the picnic today, when you and your parents went off for a private chat?"

Chapter Eight

The last thing Lulu wanted to do was tell Sam her folks' doubts about her ability to make wise decisions in her life. On the other hand, he was involved, too, if only by circumstance.

She knelt beside the wooden toy box emblazoned with the triplets' names. He knelt on the other side. Wearing a washed-till-it-was-soft cotton shirt, much the same as the one she had borrowed and was still wearing, and faded jeans, he was every inch the indomitable Texan.

Trying not to notice how sated and relaxed he looked post-lovemaking, she forced a smile and an attitude of nonchalance. "My mom and dad cornered me."

Handsome jaw tautening, he regarded her. "And?" His voice dropped another husky notch, in a way that sent heat flashing through her.

She flushed under his scrutiny. As always, his ultra-masculine presence made her feel intensely aware of him. "Bottom line? They're concerned I'm getting too involved with you and the kids."

Something flickered in his gold-flecked eyes, then maddeningly disappeared as he watched her drop more toys into the storage container.

"Is that what you think?" he asked, his expression closed and uncommunicative.

No, I think I've had the brakes on for way too long. But maybe that was the old Lulu talking. The reckless, restless, impulsive Lulu who once fell in love with Sam and ran off with him and then panicked and made the biggest mistake of her life...

The Lulu who was ruled more by emotion and the fear of disappointing anyone than logical, practical thought.

The Lulu who just gave in to the buildup from the most emotional four days of her life and recklessly made love with Sam again.

And worse, she couldn't quite bring herself to regret it. Much as the practical side of her wished that she could.

Not that he looked as if he were lamenting it, either...

Even though, as he said, none of this had to change anything between them.

When to her, it already had...

Oblivious to the conflicted nature of her thoughts, Sam persisted, "What did you say to them?"

Feeling a little unsteady, she drew a deep breath, glad to have someone to confide in about this. "I told them they were wrong," she said softly, lifting her chin. "That the kids need us both."

"They do." Finished picking up, he lifted the box and carried it over to the corner where it usually sat. Taking her by the hand, he led her to the breakfast room table. The corners of his eyes crinkled. "Which is why I've been thinking, you shouldn't just be their nanny, Lulu.

Or a concerned friend helping out." He waited for her to take a seat and then settled opposite her.

He paused to look her in the eye, then said, even more resolutely, "You should be their legal guardian, too."

Legal guardian!

She caught her breath, feeling thrilled and stunned. Still, this was awfully sudden. Too sudden, maybe?

Swallowing, she lifted a halting hand. "Sam..."

He reached across the table to take her hands in his. "I'm serious, Lulu. Your parents were right. It isn't fair for you to be so involved if you're not a guardian. So why not be a co-guardian with me? It's obvious I can't do it alone."

Lulu sighed. "Neither could I."

Sam nodded his agreement, all matter-of-fact rancher now. "Even more important, you love the kids and they love you. They need a mom." Warmth spread throughout her body as his fingers tightened on hers. "I need a partner..."

Aware his grip felt as masculine and strong as the rest of him, she withdrew her hands from his. "Are you saying that because I just put the moves on you?"

A look of hurt flashed in his eyes, then disappeared. "Our lovemaking just now has nothing to do with this."

"Doesn't it?" she returned.

He kept his gaze locked with hers. "No." His expression sobered, becoming all the more sincere. "These are two separate issues."

For him, maybe. But for her?

Her desire for him seemed an integral part of her. Aware she could fall way too hard for him if she wasn't careful, she folded her arms.

"You say that now." She drew a deep breath, wishing he weren't so sexy and capable and kind. So tender and good with the kids. "But what happens if you and I start down that road again and then don't work out as a couple again?" she challenged, feeling self-conscious, as he zeroed in on her nervousness. "How would you feel about sharing guardianship duties with me then?"

"If that happens, and I don't think it will, we'll do exactly what we're doing now and figure out how to continue to make things work—as friends," Sam said firmly. "But instinct tells me that we will work out, Lulu. And if you listen to yours, I imagine you'll be convinced of the same thing."

He was right about that. Only it wasn't her feminine instinct doing the talking. It was her heart that wanted to be with Sam and the kids...

"So what do you say, darlin'?" he proposed softly, gripping her hands again and looking deep into her eyes. "Will you be their co-guardian with me?"

Lulu might still be confused about what she wanted when it came to Sam, but there was no doubt at all about what her heart wanted in regard to the three little boys. Or what would be best for them. They needed both a mother figure and a father figure in their lives.

Joy bubbled up inside her. She'd imagined she would have to fight to make this happen. Instead, once again, she and Sam were on the exact same page.

She returned his searching gaze and said, ever so softly, "Yes, I'd love to be legally responsible for the triplets, too."

Their new deal would inadvertently solve another problem she had not been looking forward to contending with. She pushed back her chair and rose, aware it was time for them to wake the children for dinner. "This way, you won't have to pay me for caring for them."

"I'll still owe you..."

"No," she cut him off, feeling vaguely insulted by his insistence, although she wasn't sure why, "you won't."

Their stare-down continued.

"This isn't about the money, Lulu," he warned.

"I know it isn't," she agreed. "For you." But for her…the thought of him being her boss…giving her a paycheck… Well, that might have been their *initial* agreement, the only way she'd gotten herself in the door to help. Yet from the first moment the children arrived at Hidden Creek Ranch, she hadn't felt like his employee so much as she'd felt like his comrade in arms.

"But I still prefer it this way," she reiterated, "with us equally responsible. And absolutely zero money changing hands."

"I owe you…"

"And you've paid me," she stated, just as vehemently, "in room and board."

His eyes glinted, the way they always did when he let her have what she wanted. He exhaled, his gaze drifting over her with lazy male appreciation before finally returning to her face. "I'm not going to win on this. Am I, darlin'?"

"No, cowboy," Lulu shot back sassily. Knowing the only way they would ever truly be able to come together was as equals. She whirled on her heel and marched off. "You are not!"

As for the rest…

She sighed.

Sam was right. They could figure it all out later. In the meantime, the first thing they needed to do was take care of the legal formalities.

"I think that's wonderful," Hiram said when Lulu and Sam called his office the following morning, just after breakfast.

Sam looked over at Lulu, who was smiling from ear to ear. He felt relieved and happy about their new agreement, too. As far as it went, anyway. They still had a lot to work out about their own relationship, but he could be patient on that front. In the meantime, as far as the caretaking went, he and Lulu were in this together. And as they'd already more than proved, he thought, returning her excited grin, they made a very good team.

As unaware as Lulu of the romantic nature of Sam's thoughts, Hiram concluded, "I'll send the appropriate papers to Liz and Travis. You can go to their law office to sign them."

"Thank you, we will," Lulu replied.

They all signed off.

And just in time, too, Sam thought. Behind them, a cacophony of toddler voices sounded.

"Horsey!" Theo yelled.

"Me ride!" Andrew insisted.

"No! Doggy," Ethan disagreed. Not sure what was going on, since the boys had escaped to the living room while they were on the phone, Sam and Lulu headed off in their direction. They found Beauty standing parallel to the big leather sofa. Ethan was standing just in front of her and petting her face gently while Theo and Andrew tried to simultaneously climb on her back and ride her like a horse.

"Oh dear!" Lulu rushed to rescue the remarkably patient Saint Bernard.

Sam plucked both little cowboys off her back and deposited them on the far end of the sofa, out of harm's way. "Fellas, Beauty is not a horse," he scolded. "So you *cannot* climb on her back." He gave his dog a consoling pat on the head, then lifted Ethan out of the way, too. With a beleaguered sigh and the way now clear, Beauty lumbered down the hall, over to her cushion in the corner of the kitchen, and sank into the bed.

All three boys began jumping on the sofa, as hard and high as they could. "Want friends," Theo shouted loudly.

"Play now!" Andrew agreed.

"Go car," Ethan explained.

Lulu went to her phone. "I'll see if I can arrange a playdate," she called over her shoulder.

She came back five minutes later. The triplets had given up jumping but were now attempting to climb onto and slide down the bannister. Every time Sam plucked one off, another climbed on.

"Everyone is at preschool," Lulu informed him, lifting her brow at the boys. Like magic, they all stopped climbing on the stair railing. Only to resume jumping and shouting from the sofa. Lulu shouted to be heard above the bedlam. "Kelly said the triplets could be visitors in her three-year-old class today, which in the summer runs from nine to one o'clock."

Knowing the only thing that ever entertained the boys for long was other children, Sam replied, "Sounds good."

The boys were even more delighted.

While they drove to town, Lulu called their attorney and arranged to visit their office to sign the guardianship papers Hiram had sent.

"You sure you don't want to think about this?" Liz and Travis asked them, after they'd dropped the kids off.

To Sam's relief, Lulu shook her head, looking prettier and more determined than ever. "No. Sam and I agree they need both of us."

They walked out of the office building into the late-morning sunlight. For a moment, they just looked at each other. He studied the rosy color in her cheeks and the shimmer of excitement in her eyes. He was happy she was finally getting the children she had wanted, too. They were all lucky to have each other.

Her gaze swept over his form, making him glad he had taken the time to iron his shirt instead of just shave and shower and put on the first set of clean clothes he pulled from his closet.

Instead of going to the passenger side of his pickup, she remained in the sunlight. "You know," Lulu mused, "this is the first time we've been without chaperones in almost five days. I almost don't know what to do with myself."

He had to fight not to reach out and touch the silky strands of her honey-brown hair. "I know."

An awkward silence fell. He observed the pulse throbbing in her throat.

She raked her teeth across the lush softness of her lower lip. "I don't want to go too far, though, in case the triplets suddenly decide they don't want to be at preschool after all."

"No kidding," Sam said, wishing it were appropriate to take her in his arms and kiss her.

She cocked her head to one side, as if thinking the same thing. He was about to reach for her, figuring they could at least hug each other in congratulations, when Lulu's phone rang.

"Oh no," Lulu said, plucking it from her purse.

"Don't tell me it's the school already," Sam said. Which in one sense would not be surprising, since the drop-off had been almost *too* easy to be believed, with the kids going right in without batting an eye.

"No." She exhaled, looking distressed. "It's not them. It's Dan."

To Lulu's relief, Sam was happy to accompany her to the sheriff's station.

Her brother ushered them into a conference room and,

as usual, got straight to the point as soon as she and Sam sat down. "We found your bees."

Lulu had figured as much, when he'd said he had *news*. "Where are they?"

"A commercial melon farm in Wisconsin. The owner thought it was a legitimate lease. When he saw your brand listed as stolen on the state agricultural website, he notified authorities there immediately. They, in turn, contacted us."

"Thank goodness for that," Lulu said as Sam reached over and squeezed her hand. "How are my hives doing?"

Dan looked down at his notes. "Apparently, there was some loss, but the majority of the hives seem to be doing well. The question is what to do now. The farm owner still needs your bees for his crops, but he understands if you want them shipped back immediately."

Her heart racing, Lulu asked, "Do you have his contact information?"

Dan handed her a piece of paper.

Lulu called the melon farmer. They talked at length. Finally, she hung up. Her brother had gone off to attend to other law enforcement business. But Sam was still there, waiting. Patient and calm as ever.

"Everything okay?" he asked, his handsome face etched with concern.

Her emotions still in turmoil, Lulu nodded and led the way into the hall. She waved to the front desk and, aware it would soon be time to pick up the triplets, headed out into the summer sunshine. "The farm owner is going to pay the going rate, which will be negotiated through our lawyers, and keep the hives until late August."

Easing a hand beneath her elbow, Sam matched his steps to hers. "And then what?"

"I'll either ship them back home or sell them outright to a beekeeper where they are now."

Sam stopped in midstride. "You'd really do that?"

Not willingly. She also knew she had to be practical here, now that she was co-guardian to the triplets. "It might make the most sense."

"Those bees are your life's work," he reminded her, clearly disappointed.

Lulu tensed. She didn't like him judging or second-guessing her. Shifting her bag higher on her arm, she returned in a cool tone, "That's true. They were." She paused to look him straight in the eye. "But things are different now I'm going to be raising the triplets. Already, I've had to ask beekeeping friends to install a new queen for me, and tend my remaining hive on an emergency basis, because I just don't have time to get over to the ranch. That being the case, it might be better for me to pocket the cash from the sale and concentrate on the kids for now. Worry about resuming my beekeeping career later."

Sam stared at her. Feeling like he had gone back in time to their college years, when Lulu had flitted from one thing to another, changing her major almost as often as she changed hairstyles. A pattern that had continued for at least three years after the two of them had broken up.

In fact, to date, beekeeping was the one thing, the *only* thing, she seemed to have stuck with.

Her lips slid out in a seductive pout. "You don't approve?" she challenged.

He rubbed his jaw, considering. The last thing he wanted to do was make an emotional situation worse. "I know it's hard now, but I think if you give it all up you might regret it, darlin'."

Her eyes turned dark and heated. "Exactly why I'm putting off the decision for a couple of months, so I will have time to think about what I want to do."

With a scowl, she pivoted and continued on to the parking lot, walking briskly ahead of him. "I'm not going to lean on you financially, if that's what you're worried about. Whatever I decide to do, I'll have enough to pay my share of the kids' expenses. And of course all my own, too."

He caught up with her, sliding his hand beneath her elbow once again. "That's not what I'm worried about and you know it."

She whirled, coming close enough he could inhale her tantalizing floral scent and feel her body heat radiating off of her. "Then…?"

His gaze drifted over her pretty turquoise sundress and silver necklace. It was all he could do not to touch her.

Aware this was something they did need to discuss, even if it was unpleasant, he stuck his hands into the back pockets of his jeans instead. "I just wouldn't want you to change your mind about other things down the road, too."

"Like…?"

He shrugged. Was she really going to make him say it? Apparently, she was. "The kids."

Color swept into her high, sculpted cheeks. "Did you *really* just say that to me?"

"Look, I wasn't trying to insult you—"

"So you did accidentally?"

He tracked the silky spill of hair across her bare shoulders. Figuring if they were going to be co-guardians, they ought to be able to talk everything out together, he shrugged. Given what she'd just said about the business she'd spent the last seven years building…which was also the one thing, the only thing, he'd seen her feel maternal toward, up to now. "It's a legitimate worry."

Hurt sparked in her gaze. "No, it isn't, Sam," she disagreed quietly. "And if you really feel that way…"

What he really felt was the intense urge to haul her close and kiss her until the tension between them went away. The fact he'd been brought up a Texas gentleman kept him from doing so, but—

Her phone pinged to signal an incoming text.

She paused, brow furrowing, and read the screen. "It's Kelly," she said in concern. She looked up at Sam. "She said there may be trouble at the preschool. She wants us to come now to get the kids."

Fortunately, they were only a couple of minutes away. Sam climbed behind the wheel and Lulu settled in the passenger seat. He stretched his arm along the back of the seat and looked behind them as he backed his truck out of the space. He paused before he put it in gear. "She didn't say anything more?"

She shook her head. "Nope."

Sam drove through the lot and turned onto the street. Hands gripping the wheel, he asked, "You don't think they caused some sort of ruckus, do you?"

Lulu sighed, and put a hand over her eyes, looking like a harried mother. She pressed her soft lips together ruefully. "I wish I could say no, but you know how they are when they're overtired."

He did, indeed.

It seemed to take forever to make it to the school, a fact hampered by the number of cars lining up in the driveway and down the street. They bypassed the drop-off and parked. Still not speaking to each other, they headed inside.

There were no sounds of crying or wild behavior as they moved through the hall.

When they cleared the doorway to Kelly's classroom, the boys were huddled together anxiously, watching the portal. Other kids were being escorted out by their moms and dads.

"Hey, guys." Lulu knelt down to say hello. Sam hunkered down beside her. "How's it going?"

"Want *Mommy*," Theo said fiercely.

Andrew folded his arms militantly. "Want *Daddy*."

"Go *home*," Ethan said, his lower lip trembling.

Too late, Sam realized it might have been a mistake to bring them to a setting that so closely mirrored the place where they'd been when they'd received the news that something terrible had happened and their parents weren't coming back.

Sam started to engulf them in a reassuring hug. "We're going to take you home, fellas," he said.

"No!" Theo shouted, pushing him away. "Want Mommy!"

"Want Daddy," Andrew agreed, wriggling free.

"Me scared," Ethan collapsed to the floor in a limp heap and sobbed outright.

The hysteria spread. Within seconds, other preschoolers were welling up. Some sobbing. Others loudly demanding their own parents take them home. And so it went, well after the classroom was cleared.

The triplets, it seemed, weren't going anywhere. Not willingly, it seemed.

Kelly disappeared, then came back a few minutes later. "I called the head of grief counseling over at the hospital. She's on her way over now."

"Thank heavens," Lulu whispered, moving closer to Sam as if for protection while the boys clustered together on the play rug on the floor, stubbornly waiting.

Kate Marten-McCabe breezed in.

The silver-haired therapist had a small cooler and a big bag of books and toys. "I've got some things for us to do," she announced with soothing candor. She glanced at the three adults remaining. "Could y'all could give us a little time to talk? Maybe wait for us on the playground, where we'll have Popsicles later?"

Sam and Lulu nodded.

They walked to a bench beneath a shady tree in silence. "Well, you were right," Sam admitted ruefully as they took a seat side by side.

Lulu slanted him a questioning glance.

He cleared his throat. "Maybe we're both going to have to step back from our jobs for a while." He paused to look deep into her eyes, intensifying the intimacy between them. He took her hand in his and squeezed it affectionately. "And I'm sorry I didn't realize that as quickly as you did."

Lulu knew it was a big step, and an important one, for Sam to say he was wrong when they differed. He had never done so in the past. Instead, had just expected her to come around to his way of thinking or accept he wasn't going to change his opinion and deal with it.

She looked down at their entwined fingers. Realizing she could have done more to intuit the reason behind his worry and reassure him on the spot that she would never ever abandon him or the kids, rather than simply go on the defensive.

"Apology accepted," she said quietly. She turned to face him, her bent knee nudging his thigh. "But as for your work, running Hidden Creek… Could you really step back for more than a week or two?"

The reservation was back in his eyes, along with a

lingering desire she felt, too. "My foreman and the other ranch hands can handle everything day-to-day until the boys are really settled."

"That could take a while."

He exhaled roughly. "I _know_." But seemed prepared to make the sacrifice nevertheless.

Silence fell between them.

"What do you think is going on in there?" he asked finally.

Lulu turned toward the school, saw no sign of anyone coming outside. "Kate's probably explaining to them that their parents aren't coming back."

His expression turned brooding. "You think they'll accept that?"

Recalling the raw grief the triplets had exhibited, their emotional expectation that their parents would magically appear to take them home, Lulu drew in another jagged breath. She looked down at her and Sam's entwined hands. Realized they really did need each other to see the boys through this rough patch. "At their age? I don't know."

Another silence fell.

This time they didn't talk.

Finally, Kelly came out of the school with two sets of triplets, hers and theirs. All six had Popsicles. As she neared, Sam and Lulu disengaged their hands and stood.

Kelly gave them a smile. "Kate would like to talk to you inside."

They found the grief counselor in the classroom, packing up. She gestured for them to have a seat. "I explained to the boys that their parents are in heaven, but they don't really comprehend what that is yet. They just know their parents won't be coming to pick them up today." She brought a notebook and pen out of her bag. "How have the kids been doing at home?" she asked kindly.

"Better every day," Sam said.

"Is there any hyperactivity?" Kate asked.

Reluctantly, Lulu admitted, "Pretty much all the time."

"Their sleeping?"

"Fitful at best," Lulu said.

They went on to explain about the night terrors and their inability to get them to lie down in their own beds.

"In fact," Lulu added, "the only way they will rest at all, for any length of time, is if we're holding them."

Kate did not look surprised. "How is their eating?"

"They like sweets," Sam replied, "but when it comes to anything else, they're pretty picky."

Lulu nodded. "They'll ask for something, like pancakes or scrambled eggs, but then they don't really eat much of it."

"Have they had any temper tantrums?"

Sam and Lulu nodded in tandem. "At least once a day."

"These are all signs of toddler grief. Healing is going to take time. But the good news is, we have programs at the hospital for all of you that will help."

Sam and Lulu exchanged relieved glances. Feeling more like a team than ever, Lulu asked, "What can we do in the meantime?"

"Reinstate as many familiar routines from their old life as you can, including preschool. Get them on a schedule and sleeping in their own beds. Help them remember their parents and the love they received in a way that is comforting and heartwarming rather than grief-provoking. And…" Kate handed them a storybook for orphaned children and a packet of information with her card attached "…bring them to the children's grief group at the hospital on Saturday morning. The two of you can attend the one for guardians and caretakers."

"Thank you." Sam and Lulu shook her hand, promising in unison, "We will."

Kate smiled. "Call me if you have any questions or concerns." She slipped out of the classroom.

Sam and Lulu turned to face each other. Aware what a sticky situation they had found themselves in, it was hard not to feel completely overwhelmed. Especially when the two of them were still privately mourning the loss of their friends, too. "Looks like we have our hands full, cowboy," she murmured in an attempt to lighten the mood and dispel some of the grief they were both feeling.

He returned her quavering smile. "And then some." His gaze stroked her features, every one, ending with her eyes. With his customary confidence, he promised, "Together, we'll make it all work out. But first things first. You've got to move in."

Chapter Nine

Lulu gaped at Sam. His thick blond hair rumpled, his gold-flecked eyes filled with worry, he looked a little ragged around the edges. Which, after the afternoon they'd had, was exactly how she felt. And they still had the rest of the day, and night, to get through.

"You want me to actually move in?" she repeated in astonishment, not sure she'd understood him correctly. "With you?"

"And the boys, obviously," Sam said. He appeared perfectly at ease with the idea of them residing together under one roof, full-time.

"Temporarily," Lulu ascertained.

He shook his head, correcting, "From here on out."

Lulu was still trying to wrap her mind around that when he moved closer. His gaze caressed her face. "You heard what Kate said." He tucked his hand in hers, gave it a tender squeeze. "If we want the boys to recover, we have to give them as much security as possible. Get back to familiar routines." He paused to let his words sink in. Once again, a thoughtful silence brought them together.

"And what was normal to them," he continued practically, "was living with a mom and a dad under one roof."

A tingle of awareness sweeping through her, Lulu hitched in a breath. "That's true," she managed around the sudden dryness of her throat. The thought of making love with him again dominated her mind. "But..." It would be impossible to ignore their attraction for long under such intimate circumstances. A fact she guessed he knew very well!

Dropping his grip on her, he stepped back. Cocked a brow. "What?" he prodded.

This was the kind of impulsive thing *she* would do. Not him. Doing her best to control her soaring emotions, she studied him from beneath her lashes. "Are you sure you really want to do this?" Thus far, their arrangement had been only temporary. Meant to last only until the boys adjusted and were sleeping peacefully through the night.

They'd yet to discuss what would happen after that.

"If we're going to raise them together, as full-time co-guardians, we need to be *permanently* under one roof." He lifted a hand. "We could do it at your place, of course, but it's so much smaller..."

They would be tripping all over each other.

"And the boys are already sort of used to staying at Hidden Creek. I don't think it would be smart to uproot them again, do you? Especially after what happened a little while ago." He jerked his head in the direction of the classroom floor.

Aware that Kelly and the two sets of triplets were waiting for them on the playground, Lulu began moving about the classroom, gathering up the boys' things. "No. Of course it wouldn't be wise to move them again," she said.

He held her carryall open while she slid their belongings inside. "Then…?"

The two of them hesitated just inside the door. Lulu hated to admit it, but she was worried about how it would look. "If I actually move in," she murmured, looking up at him, "people are going to probably assume, because of our romantic history, that you and I are a couple again."

Sam lounged, arms folded, with one brawny shoulder braced against the wall. His glance drifted over her intimately. "So?"

"So," Lulu said before she could stop herself, "that could put a crimp in your dating life." *Oh my god! Where did that thought come from?*

To her embarrassment, her flash of jealousy did not go unnoticed.

Male satisfaction tugging at the corners of his lips, he stepped closer, gently cupped her shoulders and told her exactly what she had hoped to hear. "I'm not going to have any dating life when I have three kids to take care of."

A thrill swept through her. She forced herself to calm down. Just because they'd had a brief fling did not mean he would ever fall in love with her again, or vice versa. And from what she'd seen in the time since they'd broken up, he'd suffered no shortage of attractive female dinner companions.

Shrugging, she stepped back, away from the enticing feel of his warm, calloused hands on her bare skin. "You might be surprised. A lot of women my age have baby fever." *A lot of women lust after you.* She pretended an insouciance she couldn't begin to feel. "Three adorable toddlers could make you a very hot prospect."

Just that suddenly, something came and went in the air between them. The slightest spark of hope of renewed passion and a rekindling of the love they had once shared.

"Is that why you made love with me?" he chided, in a tone that was half joking, half serious. "Because you have a well-known case of baby fever? And wanted in on the bounty of family I suddenly found myself blessed with?"

Wondering just what it was about him that made her unable to get over him, she said, "Of course not."

To her chagrin, he looked skeptical.

"As I said before, I made love with you because I was…" *nostalgic for what we once shared*, she wanted to say "…curious," she fibbed instead.

His eyes darkened with a mixture of masculine pride and intense interest. Oblivious to the leaping of her heart, he mused in a low, husky voice that made her want to kiss him passionately, "You wanted to see if it was as good as we both recalled."

"Yes," she replied in a strangled voice.

Seemingly in no hurry to leave until he had the answers he wanted, Sam tucked a hand behind her ear. "And was it?"

Lulu swallowed around the building tightness in her throat. "Physically, you know it was." She shoved her hands into the pockets of her sundress skirt. In an attempt to appear oh-so-casual, she leaned against the bulletin board decorated with pictures of family. Children, parents, grandparents, pets… The sum of which made her want him, and everything he offered, all the more.

"And emotionally?" His gaze dropped to her lips and he came closer still.

She planted a hand on the center of his chest before she gave in to the temptation to kiss him again. "Whoa there, cowboy." She stepped aside. "I'm not going there."

Sam shrugged. And straightened. "We're going to have to eventually, if we plan to adopt the kids."

Wow. The man just didn't stop. But then, she remembered that about him, too. When he wanted something, he worked single-mindedly until he achieved his goal.

Her eyes widened. "If *we* plan to *adopt*?" she echoed.

Talk about acting impulsively and going way too far way too fast! Had the two of them exchanged personality flaws or what?

Shrugging, he straightened to his full six feet three inches. "You didn't think I'd be content to be just guardians forever. Did you?"

Honestly, she'd been so busy trying to keep pace with the swift moving events she hadn't given it any thought. Although in the back of her mind, she had always thought, if she were lucky enough to be given the chance to raise the kids, she would certainly adopt.

None of that meant, however, that she and Sam should rush into anything again. No matter how selfless the reason.

She folded her arms. "First of all, Sam, at this point, the boys are so young they don't know the difference between us being their guardians versus their adoptive parents."

"But they will, probably before we know it. And if we want to give them the most stable family possible, we should probably be married, too."

Of course he would throw in a matter-of-fact proposal. Sam was a get-things-done kind of person. He never put off for tomorrow what could be done right now.

The thing was, to her surprise, she could see them eventually deciding to get married, too, if it meant giving the three little boys more security.

Still, she had to make sure she and Sam were on the

exact same wavelength when it came to their future. That she wasn't jumping to erroneous conclusions. "And we would eventually do this as a convenience," she said, trying not to think what his steady appraisal and deep voice did to her.

"Yes. And a way to ensure sexual exclusivity."

Leave it to him, she thought with a mixture of excitement and exasperation, to spell it out when she would rather have left it undecided.

"Because you're right, Lulu," he continued in a way that seemed designed to curtail her emotional vulnerability. And maybe his, too. "If we're just living together, acting as guardians and taking care of the kids without having made a formal public commitment to each other, people will speculate about the state of our relationship."

And that could hurt the kids at some point down the road, Lulu realized.

"So, if we find we have needs…" She kept her eyes locked with his, even as her heart raced like a wild thing in her chest.

He squared his shoulders. "Then we satisfy them with each other."

It was certainly a practical, adult approach to what could be a very thorny situation. There was also no doubt they'd both lost the naivete that had once made them believe in fairy-tale romance and happy endings.

Even so, thinking about adoption and eventual marriage was a risk. One she wasn't sure she was ready to take, even if he wanted to go ahead and get everything settled. "What makes you think a marriage of convenience would work?" she challenged. Were they even really discussing this? "When our previous romance crashed and burned?" *Big-time*.

"There would be less pressure on us, as a couple and

a family, if you and I went into it from a practical standpoint, as friends and co-parents."

And less pressure, at least in his view, meant it might work.

"And maybe, at some point, lovers, too." Doing her best to protect them both, she went back to his previous point.

A corner of his mouth quirked. "Yes." He looked as pleased as she was by the prospect of never having to imagine each other with anyone else. His gaze drifted over her lovingly. "I could see that happening," he rasped, taking her hand and rubbing his thumb along the inside of her wrist, starting a thousand tiny fires. "Especially after what happened yesterday."

Lulu flushed. Their lovemaking had been spectacular. No question. All she had to do was think about what it had felt like to be with him again, and renewed need pulsed inside her. Pushing aside the lingering thrill, she cautioned, "We need to slow down, Sam. Take it one day, one step at a time."

He glanced at her, as if his heart were on the line, too. "But you'll think about it?" he pressed.

Was he kidding? She wouldn't be able to do anything but!

An hour and a half later, all three boys shouted and giggled as they bounced wildly up and down on the center of Lulu's queen-size bed.

"Whoo whee!"

"Jump!"

"Me fun!"

Keeping watch to make sure the boys remained somewhat contained and didn't tumble off the mattress, Sam asked, "Can I help you?"

Lulu could tell he wanted her to go faster. It wasn't easy to pack when she was so completely distracted.

"Yes," she said, getting a handful of frilly bras and panties from her drawer and stashing them as unobtrusively as possible in the duffel she had looped over her arm. Noting Sam's glance tracking a silky burgundy thong hanging over the side, she hastily stuffed it out of sight. In an effort to direct his attention elsewhere, she inclined her head toward the boys. "Make sure they don't fall off and land on their heads."

"Okay, guys, settle down a little bit. We don't want anyone getting hurt."

The triplets responded by hopping around even higher.

Lulu sighed. What was it about guys and danger?

"I've got this," Sam said, scooping them up into his arms. "Time to sing the monkey song!"

The boys, who'd been hyperactive since their expression of grief earlier in the day, paused. All three tilted their head at Sam.

He sat down on the bed and gathered them onto his lap. "Everybody knows the monkey song," Sam said. He sang, "One little monkey jumping on the bed. He fell off and bumped his head. Momma called the doctor and the doctor said…" he wagged his finger in theatrical admonishment "…no more monkeys jumping on the bed!"

The boys began to grin. Clearly, they'd heard this children's song before.

He glanced over at her. "You could join in."

Still gathering shirts, shorts, pajamas and the occasional summer dress or skirt, Lulu winked at the guys in her life and, as requested, added her voice to Sam's baritone. "Two little monkeys…"

The boys chimed in, too, their words and tune garbled and mostly nonsensical but cute.

To Lulu and Sam's mutual relief, the switch in activity helped bring about much needed calm. They were up to ten monkeys by the time Lulu had what she needed for the rest of the week in two clothes baskets.

"Sure that's all?" Sam asked when she showed him what he would need to carry down to her Lexus for her while she shepherded the boys outside.

"Yep."

He quirked a brow.

She knew what he was thinking. If she was really moving in, she should be taking a lot more with her. For lots of reasons she preferred not to examine too closely, she needed to keep one foot out the door. Leaving the majority of her summer clothes at the Honeybee Ranch would accomplish that.

That evening, they closely followed their nighttime routine. Dinner, bath and then, at long last, story time. With Lulu and Sam sitting side by side on the sofa and all three boys sprawled across their laps, they read a few of the favorite tales. Then injected the book Kate Marten-McCabe had given them, about children whose parents had gone to heaven.

The boys listened, but did not seem to connect it to Peter and Theresa or themselves.

Sam and Lulu continued reading, alternating stories, until the boys fell asleep, then carried them one by one upstairs to their toddler beds.

With the boys asleep, Sam went to take Beauty out while Lulu stayed nearby, putting her things away. Shortly after Sam returned, the boys awakened. And once again, Sam and Lulu walked the floor with them, only to end up for the rest of the night snuggled with all five of them together in Sam's big bed, Beauty sleeping on the floor next to them.

The following morning, as per Kate's advice, they went into town and formally enrolled the boys in preschool, from nine to one o'clock every day.

"So what's next on the list Kate gave us?" Sam asked as they walked out of the preschool.

Relieved the drop-off had been so easy and feeling a lot like the co-parents they aspired to be, Lulu fell into step beside him. "We need to find a way to help the boys remember Peter and Theresa."

Sam matched his long strides to her shorter ones. "All their belongings are in the boxes in my attic."

Lulu pushed aside the dread she felt at having to tackle such an emotional chore. They had to do this for the kids. "Want to go have a look?"

He nodded.

Like the rest of Sam's home, the third floor of the ranch house was clean, well lit and spacious. They pulled the boxes to the rug on the center of the wood floor and wordlessly began going through them, finding clothes of Theresa's and Peter's. A huge cache of old photos. Theresa's perfume. Peter's aftershave. Photos of their Memphis elopement.

"Here's a few with us in the picture, too," Sam said thickly. He handed over a photo of the four of them. The guys were in suits and ties, the gals in pretty white spring dresses. The guys wore boutonnieres, the girls carried bouquets.

"We were so young," Lulu murmured.

"And happy and idealistic," Sam said, studying their smiling faces.

If only they could have stayed that way, Lulu thought wistfully. But they hadn't, so...

She handed the photo back to Sam. And took out another. This one of Peter and Theresa at the hospital with their three newborns. Their first Christmas, the boys' first and second birthdays. One from Easter that year, which had to have been taken just before Theresa and Peter's death. A folder of the children's artwork from school. Another with newspaper articles detailing the eight-car pileup on the Houston freeway during morning rush hour that had killed them and seriously injured a dozen others.

Suddenly, the loss was too much. The grief hit Lulu hard, and she began to cry.

"Hey," Sam said, folding her close. After reading the articles, his eyes were wet, too. "Hey…" He stroked a hand through her hair. "I've got you…"

Needing the comfort only he could give, she snuggled into the reassuring safety of his strong arms. "Oh, Sam," she sobbed. "This is all just so unfair!" Her chin quivering, tears still streaming down her face, she struggled to get her emotions under control. "How are we ever going to fill the void their parents' deaths have left?"

Sorrow etched the handsome contours of Sam's face. "The only way we can," he countered, cupping her face between his big hands. "By taking it one day, one moment at a time. And becoming a real family in every possible way."

Lulu thought of the boys' meltdown the previous day, their sad little faces, the heartrending sounds of their sobs when they awakened at night.

"But what if we fail them?" she asked, knowing she'd never been so scared and so overwhelmed. "The way we once failed each other?"

Chapter Ten

"We're not going to fail them, darlin'," Sam said.

The depth of her despair only made her look more vulnerable. He wiped away her tears, cuddling her even closer. Still caging her loosely in his arms, he gently kissed her temple. "We never fail when we're together. It's only when we split up that we make a mess of things."

For a brief second, she seemed to take his assertion at face value. Then worry clouded her eyes. "I wish I shared your confidence."

But she didn't. She didn't believe in herself. In him. Or in the two of them.

So he showed her the only way he could what an excellent team they made. Determined to convince her, he lowered his mouth to hers and delivered a deep and sensual kiss. As he hoped, she opened herself up to his embrace just as swiftly. Wreathing her arms about his neck, she let out an involuntary moan and curled against him. Returning the hot, riveting kiss again and again and again. Blood rushing hot and needy through his veins, he slid his hands beneath her shirt and her nipples pearled against the centers of his palms.

"Oh, Sam," Lulu whispered, as he trailed kisses along the shell of her ear, down the nape of her neck. The tears she'd shed still damp across her face.

She whimpered, another helpless little sound that sent his senses swimming even more. Aware he had never wanted a woman as much as he wanted her, he deepened the kiss. Her mouth was pliant beneath his, warm and sexy, her body soft, surrendering. And still they kissed, sweetly and languidly, hotly and passionately, slowly and tenderly. Until worries faded and pleasure reigned.

Not about to take advantage, though, Sam reluctantly drew back. "Now's the time," he teased, looking deep into her eyes. "Tell me to stop." He caressed the damp curves of her lip with his fingertip. "Or go."

Her turquoise eyes smoldered. "Go," she said, smiling and taking him by the hand and leading him down the stairs, away from everything that had been so upsetting, to her bedroom. She shut the door behind them. She plucked a brand-new box of condoms from the nightstand drawer.

"Definitely go." She shimmied out of her skirt. Drew her blouse off, too.

"Gotta say," he drawled, enjoying the view of her in a peach bra and panties set, knowing she had obviously planned ahead. "I like the way this is going." The fact she'd known, just as he had, that despite all the problems still facing them, they would make love again.

She toed off her sandals. "Good." She motioned toward his clothes. "Your turn, cowboy."

Appreciating the reckless, sexy side of her, he stripped down to his boxers.

Her delicate brow lifted. "Keep going."

He didn't need to glance down to know he was getting pretty far ahead of her. "Ah...sure?"

Mischief and her typical zest for life sparkled in her smile. Tilting her head to one side, she gave him a lusty once-over. "Mmm-hmm."

"What the lady wants." He obliged and saw her eyes go wide.

Rationally, Lulu knew they shouldn't be making love again, at least not so soon, when the last time he'd been so casual, and she'd felt so inexplicably conflicted, afterward. But for now, as she sauntered toward him, took him in her arms and kissed him again, all she could think about was how much every one of them had been through in such a brief span of time, how short life was. How unpredictable. The only thing she could count on, besides this very moment they were in, was how good she felt whenever she was with him. How grateful that they had found each other again.

With a low murmur of appreciation, Sam stopped kissing her long enough to ease off her bra and panties. Her hands rested on his shoulders while he helped her step out. Still kneeling, he savored the sight of her, then kissed her most sensitive spot. She quivered, clinging to him like a lifeline, aware that she was on the brink.

He left her just long enough to retrieve a condom and then roll it on. Then he settled her against the wall. She wrapped her legs around his waist and they were kissing again. Touching. Caressing. Finding and discovering every pleasure point.

She was wet and open. He was hot and hard. So hard.

And then there was no more waiting. He surged inside her and she welcomed him home. All was lost in blazing passion and overwhelming need. Pleasure spiraled. Soared. And then they floated blissfully down into a satisfaction unlike anything she had ever known.

Afterward, they clung together, still pressed up against the wall, their bodies still entwined and shuddering with release. Eventually, he let her down. Sam kissed her shoulder tenderly as her feet touched the floor, and she continued leaning up against him, snuggled into the warm, strong embrace of his arms. "Feeling better?" Sam asked.

Suddenly realizing that she and Sam and their three little boys might comprise the perfect family after all, Lulu murmured against his shoulder, "Always, when we make love."

"Same here." Sam gave her another angel-soft kiss, then drew back just far enough to see her face. "Anything else on your mind?"

"I was thinking about what you said, about us never failing when we're together."

He tucked a strand of hair behind her ear. "It's true."

Lulu thought about what else she had learned from growing up McCabe. Mindful of the time, she eased away from him and began to dress. "When you add the reality that the foundation of every happy family is the relationship of the couple at its heart." She drew a deep, bolstering breath, as she shimmied into her panties. "It makes sense that we need to be united in every way we can be."

Sam pulled on his boxers and stepped behind her to help her fasten her bra. Grinning, he said, "Including bed?"

Lulu sighed luxuriantly. "Definitely including bed. Though I'm still not sold on the two of us actually getting married in order to make that happen," she cautioned candidly while she pulled on her blouse.

Sam tensed, as if an old wound was reopened. "Because you don't want to be married to me?"

Lulu flushed self-consciously, warning herself she had nothing to feel guilty about as long as she was being completely honest with him. "Because I don't think that legal formality is even necessary these days," she clarified.

An indecipherable emotion came and went in Sam's eyes.

"But," she went on with heartfelt enthusiasm, "I am definitely on board with co-adopting the children with you." She paused to look him in the eye. "And I want to start that process as soon as possible."

To get things moving, Sam called their attorneys that same afternoon. Liz and Travis agreed to meet with Lulu and Sam the following day while the triplets were in preschool. Their two attorneys listened while Sam and Lulu outlined their plans, occasionally exchanging lawyerly looks and appearing concerned about the speed with which Lulu and Sam had reached their decision.

"Travis and I understand you want to protect the triplets," Liz said gently. "But there is a big difference between being co-guardians and adoptive parents, at least in terms of the court."

"Meaning?" Lulu asked nervously.

Sam reached over and squeezed her hand. A week ago, Lulu would have pulled away. However, today, feeling like they were members of the same family unit, she relaxed into his reassuring grip.

Both their attorneys noticed. Sobering all the more, Travis said, "To become a guardian, when you've been named by the parents in their will, is a fairly simple matter. You express a willingness to do so, papers are signed, and it's a done deal. Unless of course, there is some obvious reason why it shouldn't happen."

"But when you petition to adopt," Liz continued where her husband left off, "you have to complete a formal application and petition the court, undergo home studies and background checks."

"What are they looking for?" Sam asked.

Liz spread her hands. "Any signs of potential problems. Or instability."

"You mean mental instability?" he asked, perplexed.

"Or personal," Liz explained. "Like if someone's had multiple marriages or ones that only lasted a day, has been consistently fired from or quit their jobs, things like that…"

Lulu froze.

Travis jumped in. "Everything is looked at. Your finances, your family histories, your lifestyle. You have to provide character references and show proof of any marital history or divorce. It's a lot to undergo. Particularly when you already have your hands full just trying to acclimate the kids to their new circumstances."

Liz lifted a soothing hand. "It's not that we're expecting anything problematic to come up."

Unable to prevent herself from worrying, Lulu tried to figure out how to ask the question without revealing what she was really stressed about. "But what if it did? What if there were, I don't know, say, unpaid parking tickets? Or a noise violation?" *Or other evidence of reckless behavior.* "From years ago?"

Sam turned to look at Lulu. Poker-faced, but concerned.

"Then we'd address it," Liz said soothingly.

"But of course it would be better if we knew about any

potential issues before making any formal application or getting social services involved," Travis said.

"Agreed." Sam suddenly looked every bit as on edge as Lulu felt. Still, he sounded calm when he added, "Which is why we should probably go ahead and have your law firm do complete background checks on both of us. Just so we can see what does come up, and if there is anything, deal with it."

"I agree with Sam." Lulu did her best to mimic Sam's laid-back attitude.

Liz and Travis seemed a little surprised by their request, but readily agreed.

Trying not to look at Sam, for fear she would give away what it was they were both trying like hell to hide, Lulu asked, "How long will it take?"

Travis shrugged. "Depends on how far back you want our investigator to go."

"As far back as they can," Sam said. He was no longer looking at Lulu, either.

Travis made a note on the legal pad in front of him. "Probably seven to ten days."

"Relax." Liz smiled. She got up to walk them out. "Knowing the two of you and your squeaky-clean reputations, I'm sure it will be fine."

But would it? Given Lulu and Sam's rocky romantic past?

Sam looked over at her as they left their attorneys' office. "I think we need to talk."

"I agree."

They walked over to The Cowgirl Chef and picked up a couple of cold drinks—a mocha frappé for her and a black iced coffee for him—and then headed for the park in the center of town. As they moved across the grass toward one of the benches in the shade, Lulu sent him an anxious glance. "Do you think that what happened in Tennessee is likely to come up?"

Sam sat down beside her and draped his arm along the back of the bench. He kept his voice low as she settled beside him. "No idea if it will or not, darlin', since there was never any follow-through on our part and therefore nothing put on record. But it will probably be good to know for sure."

Lulu worked her straw back and forth between her fingertips. "What about my business? The theft I just had?" She took a long sip of her drink, then dropped her hand and ran her fingertip along the hem of her pretty cotton skirt. It had ridden up above her knee and showed several inches of bare, silky skin. "Will that make me look irresponsible for not having had a security system installed on the property?"

He moved his gaze upward, past the scoop-necked knit top cloaking her slender midriff and the swell of her breasts, to the flushed pink color in her face. She had put her honey-brown hair up in a neat knot on the back of her head before the meeting. She looked beautiful and kissable and frustrated as all get-out. He moved his hand from the back of the bench to cup her shoulder gently.

"It's Laramie County, Lulu. We don't usually need security systems here since pretty much everyone who resides here is honest and neighborly. The court will understand that."

She shifted toward him, her bare knee brushing up against his jean-clad thigh. "Yes, but will they understand I haven't decided whether or not I even want all my bees back?"

"The court will probably want to know what your plans are in that regard. If you decide not to work, at least for now in order to take better care of the kids, I'm sure the court would be okay with that. Especially since we can well afford to take care of them on my income alone."

Lulu met his eyes, then shifted forward again. "I know but I really don't want to look like a dilettante. And we both know, during college and for a couple years after, I was pretty flighty."

Sam liked the idea of her leaning on him, even if it was just for moral support. "And you worked through that and built a business to be proud of. I really don't see it as a problem."

Shame flushed her cheeks. "I really don't want anyone to find out about the choices we made on spring break."

"Hopefully, they won't."

Lulu crossed her arms beneath the soft curves of her breasts and took another sip of her coffee. "And if they do?"

He paused, taking in the anxious twist of her lips. Unlike her, he didn't regret what they had done, not then and not now, just how they had let it end. But he had been older at the time of what she had once referred to as Their Big Mistake.

He squeezed her shoulder. Knowing he would do whatever he had to do to protect her, he leaned down to whisper in her ear. "Then we'll deal with it, Lulu. The best way we know how."

"Well, there's one good thing about having the kids in preschool five half days a week," Lulu said the following morning. They'd returned to the ranch after drop-off, ready to tackle that day's To Do list. "It gives us time to do the things we couldn't do otherwise."

Sam followed her up to the second floor. "Which would normally be sleep," he joked.

"No kidding." Lulu walked into the boys' room, where the beds were still unmade. She reached for the covers on one bed. Sam, another. "I never thought I'd want just *one* solid night of shut-eye so badly."

Looking sexy as could be in a T-shirt and jeans, he arranged blankets and stuffed animals against the pillows. "That's what being a parent is all about, isn't it?" He straightened and waggled his eyebrows at her. "Losing sleep? For the best possible reason?"

To comfort them. And each other. Speaking of which… Lulu glided into Sam's arms. Hugged him fiercely. "I love those little guys."

Squeezing her back, he rasped, "So do I." They stayed that way another long moment. Sam stole a few kisses, as Lulu knew he would. Then gave her another long, affectionate hug. "Now, if we could just figure out how to get them sleeping through the night, in their own bed," he murmured against her hair.

Lulu thought for a moment. "Maybe it would help if we set up their bedroom more like it used to be. We have photos." She went to get some.

Sam studied the layout with her. "Definitely worth a try."

Together, they shifted the three toddler beds from the U shape they had been in, with the beds pushed up along the sides of the bedroom, into a neat dormitory-style row, with all the headboards against the same wall. They took the rocker glider out of the corner, as well as the box of toys, and put both out into the upstairs hall for later rearranging.

Hands on her hips, Lulu studied their handiwork, lamenting, "They won't be able to play in here at all."

Sam moved behind her. He wrapped his arms around her and rested his chin on the top of her head. "Well, maybe that was the idea," he said, bringing her softer form back against his hard body. He pressed a kiss into the top of her hair, the shell of her ear. "Theresa and Peter wanted their bedroom to be a dedicated sleeping space and nothing more."

"Maybe." Lulu leaned against Sam another long moment, then went over to stack their bedtime storybooks on top of the room's lone bureau containing their clothing. Among them was the one Kate Marten-McCabe had given them.

Sam frowned, and, as was happening more and more these days, seemed to read her mind. "I know the grief specialists said reading this to the kids would help," he ruminated, "but I get the feeling they think it's just another story, and one they don't really want to hear."

"I know what you mean." Lulu sighed. "I don't think they make the connection between their own grief and the loss the little boy and girl in the storybook experience."

Sorrow clouded Sam's eyes. "Me, either."

For a long moment, neither of them spoke.

"Maybe it will come in time," he offered finally.

"And maybe," Lulu said, knowing they needed more than hope, they needed action, "what we really need is a book about the boys and their journey."

Crinkling his brow, he walked over to look at the book she was holding. "You mean superimpose their pictures and names in this storybook?"

"Actually, I think we should go one better." Lulu gestured for Sam to follow her and walked into the guest room she was using, where she had stashed several of the boxes of old photos and mementos.

"Maybe we should put together a story about Peter and Theresa. How they fell in love. Had the triplets. And all lived together happily. And then there was an accident. Their parents went to heaven. The boys went to stay with a number of other people. Before they ended up with the two of us and Beauty."

Sam ran his palm across his jaw. "So they would understand."

Eager to get him fully on board with the idea, she clamped her hands on his biceps. "Maybe we could end it with them blowing kisses at their parents in heaven, and their parents looking down on them, happy they are okay. So they can see there is still, and will always be, some connection."

"That could work." Sam grinned down at her, his enthusiasm building.

"It *will* work," Lulu said. Happy she and Sam were becoming such a good team, she rose on tiptoe and kissed his cheek.

He squeezed her waist affectionately. "Then let's get to it!" he said.

Lulu downloaded self-publishing software that helped her write and format the custom story that evening, after the kids were asleep, while Sam sorted through the photos, selecting the ones she needed.

Together, they put the book together, and while it would never make bestseller status, it did explain with words and pictures how many people loved the triplets and how they had come to live at Hidden Creek Ranch.

They printed it out, took it into town the following day to have it laminated and bound at the copy shop, and read it to them that evening after their baths. Sam and Lulu sat together with the three boys sprawled across their laps, the homemade storybook held out in front of them.

"Again," Theo said enthusiastically when Lulu had finished.

Ethan pointed to the photos of Theresa and Peter. "Mommy," he said. "Daddy!"

Andrew leaned his head on Sam's shoulder. "Heaven," he murmured.

Beauty, who had been stretched out at their feet, sat up. As she looked from one triplet to another, she seemed to be offering comfort and condolence.

The only problem was, all three boys wanted to take the new book to bed with them. To the point where there was almost a free-for-all.

"Hang on, guys," Lulu said, rushing off. She returned with a photo of Peter and Theresa for each of them. "Would you like to sleep with these tonight?" she said.

Three little heads nodded.

"Okay, then, up you go." Sam picked up Ethan and Andrew. Lulu hefted Theo in her arms. They went up the stairs.

Although the new bedroom arrangement hadn't done much to relax the boys the night before, they weren't giving up. Lulu put on a CD of lullabies she had found in one of the moving boxes. As the soft orchestral music filled the room, the boys perked up, listening, then snuggled down on their pillows, photos, stuffed animals and blankets in their arms.

Sam sat, his back to the wall, between beds one and two, while Lulu planted herself between beds two and three.

The boys continued listening. Child by child, eyes shuttered closed.

Sam and Lulu turned on the monitor and eased from the room.

"We should do more of this," she whispered. "Helping them remember, like Kate suggested. I think it really might help."

Sam took her hand and led her down the hall. He bussed her cheek. "Maybe you and I should do some remembering, too."

Chapter Eleven

"What are we going to be remembering?" Lulu asked, her heart fluttering in her chest. The look in his eyes was so incredibly romantic!

Sam walked into his bedroom, shut the door and turned on the monitor on the bedside table. Then, pivoting back to her, he lifted her up, so she was sitting on his bureau, arms wrapped around his neck, his strong, hard body ensconced in the open V of her legs. The insides of her thighs rubbed the outsides of his. "Our first date," he murmured.

She trembled as his palms molded her breasts through the knit of her shirt and the lace of her bra, his thumbs rubbing over the tender crests. His mouth hovered above hers and Lulu felt herself surge to life.

"Our first kiss," he whispered as their lips met in a melding of want and need.

Yearning spiraled through her and she ran her hands

through his hair, giving back, meeting him kiss for kiss. The feel of his mouth on hers imbuing her with the kind of love she had wanted all her life. The kind of love only he could give.

She kissed him passionately, adoring the way his tongue stroked hers, once and then again and again, all while he never stopped touching her. Caressing her breasts, the curve of her hips, cupping her buttocks in his palms, before moving around to trace the lines of her pelvic bones and the sensitive area between her thighs.

Aware it was her turn, Lulu reached between them to unclasp his belt. Dropping hot kisses along his neck, she slid her hand inside his jeans. Felt the velvety heat and hardness, even as his mouth moved on hers in a way that was shattering in its possessive sensuality. "The first time I touched you," Lulu whispered, when they finally came up for air.

He found his way beneath her panties. "And the first time I touched you."

Deciding it was time they both got naked, she lifted his shirt over his head and tossed it aside. Taking a moment to admire him, she let her glance sift over his bare chest. His skin was golden and satiny smooth, covered with curling tufts of golden-brown hair that spread across his pecs, before angling down toward his navel. Lower still, his hardness pressed against the front of his jeans. "The first time we were together all night, in Tennessee."

Sam grinned, recalling. He helped her off with her shirt, bra, skirt. "If I could do that entire trip over, I would."

Lulu lifted up enough so he could dispense with her panties. "So would I," she admitted huskily, as the rest of his clothing followed suit. He came back to her once again, and she wound her arms about his neck. "But I'd make sure we had a different ending this time." One rife with love and tenderness, instead of heartbreak and anger.

Sam smiled over at her in a way that made her feel beautiful inside and out. He tucked an errant strand of hair behind her ear. "We may not be able to go back in time and have a do-over," he said, kissing her thoroughly and claiming her as his. "But we can certainly put all our mistakes behind us and start fresh again."

Lulu luxuriated in the feel of his mouth on hers. "I'd like that, Sam," she whispered back, pulling him close once again. "I really would…"

Sam knew Lulu was still afraid their reconciliation would turn out to be short-lived. But *he* knew better. He'd lost her once; he wasn't going to make the same mistake again. He set about showing her that he was in this for the long haul as they resumed kissing again, long and deep, soft and slow, sweet and tender.

She ran her hands over his back, across his hips. He luxuriated in the soft, silky feel of her. Caressing, exploring, entering and withdrawing in slow, shallow strokes that soon had her arching against him, clamoring for more.

And still they kissed. Taking up the rhythm he started. Until their breath caught and their hearts thundered in unison, and there was no more playing and delaying. She held fast, claiming him as he claimed her. Giving and taking everything. Tumbling into the sweet, hot abyss.

Afterward, they snuggled together, the aftershocks every bit as potent as their lovemaking had been. "This was nice." She sighed, looking utterly fulfilled as they moved from bureau to bed.

Aware he felt the same, he lay on his back. With her draped over top of him, her head nestled against his chest, he stroked a hand languidly down her spine. "Ah. You mean Sam-and-Lulu time?" he teased. Knowing he never wanted to be without her again.

She bantered back, "Where we see to our own...very adult...needs."

Realizing she looked for comfort from him as much as he yearned to receive it from her, Sam nodded. A contemplative silence fell. Moments drew out. He could feel Lulu drifting away from him, the way she usually did when her guard went back up, but he was determined not to let their closeness fade. "What are you thinking, darlin'?" Sam rasped, still enjoying how beautiful and utterly ravished she looked.

Lulu drew the sheet up over her breasts and rolled onto her side, facing him. Her honey-brown hair spilling over her shoulders, she rested her arm on the mattress and propped her head up on her hand. She met his gaze equably and drew in a bolstering breath. "That maybe we should just stop fighting our attraction to each other and accept it."

Glad she'd told him what was eating away at her, he traced the curve of her lips with his fingertip. "I haven't been fighting mine."

"I know." Their glances met, held. Her turquoise eyes sparkled ruefully. "But up to now, cowboy, I have."

How well he knew that! He took her free hand and lifted it to his mouth. Gently kissing her knuckles, he felt comfortable enough to ask, "Any particular reason why?"

She wrinkled her nose at him and let out a beleaguered sigh. "I just don't want either of us to be disappointed if things don't work out in the end."

The fact that she was beginning to feel the kind of heartfelt emotion that had drawn them to each other in the first place, in addition to the sizzling physical attraction that had always existed between them, made Sam very happy. To his frustration, however, beneath her outward pragmatism and acceptance, Lulu still seemed somewhat ambivalent.

Up one moment. And fully on board with their increasing intimacy. Wary—and down—the next.

"You don't sound deliriously pleased with the situation," he deadpanned, trying to make light of the maelstrom of emotions running through him.

"No, it's not that at all," Lulu explained. "I've just been trying really hard to keep our situation from becoming overly complicated." She shifted slightly, and the sheet moved lower, giving him a seductive glimpse of her breasts.

He felt himself grow hard again.

She raked her teeth across her lower lip and shyly admitted, "And I don't want us to have expectations of each other that we can't possibly meet, the way we did before."

He could see why she didn't want them to be disappointed in each other. Again. But it bothered him that she always expected less of them than they were capable of giving.

Still, this was progress. It was the first time they'd made love that she had expressed acceptance instead of worry or regret, at least since they had come together to care for the triplets.

"So." She waggled her brows at him mischievously, looking happy and relaxed again. "As long as this is good…for the both of us…"

"We can make love however, whenever, wherever you want," Sam promised her gently, folding her close. And as her body began to respond to the urgency of his, he made love to her all over again.

Saturday morning, Lulu and Sam attended the grief group for parents of orphaned children. As was her custom with new attendees, psychologist Kate Marten-McCabe asked them to stay after for a few minutes. "So how are things going?" the silver-blond therapist asked.

"Better." Lulu explained what they had done thus far to help the children remember their parents.

"The storybook sounds wonderful." Kate smiled.

"We still can't get them to spend the night in their own beds though," Sam said.

"Although we did get them to actually go to sleep in their beds last night," Lulu added.

"It'll come," Kate promised, and then gave them a few more tips.

"Kate's right," Lulu's brother Jack said. Sam, Lulu and the triplets had stopped by his home for lunch and an afternoon playdate with his three little girls and Jack's old friend, rehab nurse Bess Monroe. "Progress does come. But it's often in infinitesimal degrees."

"Are you trying to encourage me or discourage me?" Lulu joked while making lunch with Bess. Her famous honey-grilled chicken salads for the adults, PB&J and apple slices for the kids.

Sam and Jack stood in the doorway of the kitchen and kept an eye on the six nicely playing kids. "I'm just saying the sleep thing is a hard thing to work out," Jack retorted, sadness creasing his face.

Concerned, Lulu went over to hug her brother. His surgical skills were legendary among the returning veterans that he and Bess both helped. However, he was not so great at dealing with the grief left by the death of his wife, Gayle.

Lulu stepped back to take him in. "Are you okay?"

"It's Father's Day," Bess put in.

Jack shot her a massively irritated look.

She raised both hands. "Well, it is. You get like this every year."

Lulu turned back to Jack. "Why would this make you sad? Your children love you! I'm sure they made you gifts at school."

"They do and did," Bess put in.

Pushing aside his usual stoicism, Jack said thickly, "It's just that Father's Day reminds me of Mother's Day. Which makes me think about Gayle. And all the holidays she's never going to celebrate with us."

Lulu understood, and she knew Sam did, too. Her eyes suddenly glistening, Bess slipped from the room. She disappeared down the hall and into the bathroom. Which was no surprise, Lulu noted, since Bess and Gayle had been very good friends.

Lulu wrapped Jack in another consoling hug. "I miss her, too," she admitted, tears welling.

Sam walked over to clap Jack on the shoulder. "We all do. She was a real force of nature."

A recuperative silence fell.

Seconds later, Bess emerged. Her nose was red and her eyes too bright, but she had a cheerful smile plastered on her face. Completely ignoring what had just happened, she asked, "What do you all think? Should we eat lunch inside or outside?"

The rest of the afternoon went pleasantly. Mostly because the kids played well and the adults avoided talk of anything the least bit sensitive or uncomfortable.

As they were getting the kids ready to leave, Jack took Lulu and Sam aside. "About the nighttime travails... My only advice is to comfort them when they wake and then always put them back in their own beds for the remainder of the night, even if it means you're stretched out on the floor next to them, so they get the idea that *their* beds are for sleeping, not yours. Unless it's very special circumstances, like they're running a fever or there's a big thunderstorm or something."

"And that works?" Lulu asked as Bess came to stand next to Jack.

Jack smiled. "It does."

The events of the day stayed with Lulu.

On the way back to Hidden Creek, Lulu said to Sam, as casually as possible, "Hey. What do you think about stopping by the Honeybee and letting me and the kids off for a few minutes, and then you going and getting lost for, oh, an hour or so?"

He slanted her a quick glance. Clad in his usual snug jeans, custom-fitted boots and solid-colored cotton shirt, he looked so ruggedly masculine and handsome it was enough to make her go weak in the knees. "You serious?"

She shrugged and checked out the kids in the rearview mirror. They were all wearing their bucket hats and sunglasses, looking cute as could be, and were surprisingly wide-awake. "You must have some stuff to check on at your ranch."

"Tons."

Which was no surprise, Lulu thought. Since they'd taken custody of the triplets, Sam had been all kids, all the time.

He made the turn into the Honeybee Ranch and drove up to the house. He put the pickup in Park, then turned to look at her with a mixture of curiosity and affection. "You sure you can handle them by yourself?"

She was going to have to if she wanted to succeed with her secret plan. Lulu smiled. "Yep."

Sam reached over to cup her face in one hand. He rubbed his thumb across the curve of her cheekbone.

Said admiringly, "Your older brother sure did infuse you with confidence."

Tingling all over, Lulu smiled back at him. "And good ideas," she said mysteriously.

As Lulu expected, the boys were delighted to sit at her kitchen table and play with the kids' craft stuff that she kept for her preschool-age nieces and nephews when they visited. The triplets were covered with washable glue and glitter and colorful markers and still working on their "projects" when Sam came back an hour later.

"Surprise!" they shouted in unison. "Happy Day!"

They rushed at him, wet and sticky artwork in tow. "Here! For you! Sam!"

Looking surprised and touched, Sam hunkered down and wrapped them all in a hug. "You fellas did all this for me?"

For the second time that day, Lulu felt herself welling up. She edged closer to indulge in the group embrace. Knelt down. "Even though we're technically still guardians, they wanted you to know what a fabulous father figure you've become to them," she said hoarsely.

Sam wrapped an arm about her waist and drew her in close. He pressed a kiss to the top of her head. "Right back at you, darlin'."

One day, they would be Mommy and Daddy. But for now, Lulu thought, returning Sam's warm hug and cuddling the boys, this life they'd fashioned was more than enough.

Chapter Twelve

"Congratulations." Lulu toasted Sam three days later.

Aware how right it all felt, having her and the boys in his home, he clinked his coffee mug against hers. Who would have thought the five of them could become a family so fast? Or that mornings would become so blissful? "To you, too, darlin'."

"Can you believe it?" she whispered. Fresh from the shower and clad in yellow linen shorts, a striped tee and sneakers, she looked pretty and ready to take on their day. "The boys spent the whole night in their beds!"

His gaze drifted over her appreciatively. She'd put on makeup sparingly. Damp honey-brown hair twisted in a knot on the back of her head, she smelled of the citrus-and-flowers shampoo and soap she favored. Lower still, he could see her sleek and sexy legs.

Doing his best to tamp down his desire and focus on the conversation at hand, he lingered next to her. Enjoying their camaraderie, he leaned over to buss the top of her head and reminded her, "We did have to go back in and sit propped against the wall next to them, twice, to get them to fall back asleep."

"I know," she acknowledged. As she shifted toward him, the soft swell of her breasts rubbed against his arm. She stepped back to gaze up at him, and the absence of her touch had him feeling bereft. "But they stopped crying almost immediately and we didn't have to pick them up and walk the floor with them to calm them down. All we had to do was reassure them."

He nodded with a depth of parental satisfaction that surprised him and set his coffee mug aside. "It was a lot better than it ever has been."

She put her own mug down, then splayed her hands across his chest. "Jack's advice is really working."

He wrapped his arms around her waist and tugged her so they were touching in one long, tensile line. Burying his face in her hair, he thought of all they'd managed to accomplish in just under two weeks. Then murmured, "A lot of things are really working out."

She drew back. Smiling, she looked up at him as if she were tempted to kiss him. Would have, if not for the three little boys playing in the adjacent room.

Later, he promised himself.

They would make up for lost time. And when they did, she would understand how much she meant to him.

As she gazed up at him, a wealth of feelings was in her eyes. He realized he had never seen her looking so happy. "Oh, by the way." She snapped her fingers. "I almost forgot. It's show-and-tell at the preschool this morning."

"They have that for two-year-olds?"

Lulu slipped out of the loose circle of his arms. She grabbed the three insulated lunch sacks they'd purchased for the boys, then opened up the fridge, removed three drinks and three premade PB&J sandwiches. Before he could get there to assist, she closed the door with a sexy swivel of her hip.

"Half the kids in their group are nearly three," she said.

"Oh. Right." Knowing they needed individual packs of graham crackers and dried fruit the boys were convinced was candy, Sam got those out of the pantry and added them to the bags. Noting what a good team they made, he went to get the school backpacks, too.

"Anyway." Lulu paused to match the lunch bags to the right backpacks. Finished, she and Sam zipped them all shut. "I talked to the kids yesterday after school, while you were out talking to your foreman, about what they were going to bring today to show their classmates."

Motioning for him to follow, she strode into the adjacent playroom. "Boys! Remember? It's show-and-tell today. So, do you want to get the toys you picked out?"

Three little heads tilted. They looked up at her, seeming slightly puzzled.

Sam sympathized. For a two-year-old, what happened yesterday might as well have been eons ago. They were usually so "in the moment."

Looking sweet and maternal, Lulu knelt to their level. Gently, she reminded them, "Ethan, you were going to take your stuffed panda bear. Andrew, you were going to take your Frisbee. And, Theo, you were going to take the wall you made with your snap-together building set."

The triplets turned to each other, once again communicating visually the way only multiples could. "No," they said firmly in unison.

All three went over to their beloved Saint Bernard,

who was sprawled out on the floor, as per usual, watching over them.

"Take Beauty!" they chorused.

"Ah, guys," Sam said reluctantly, hunkering down. He hated disappointing them. "I'm sorry," he informed them as kindly as he could. "But that's not possible."

"Take Beauty!" they shouted again.

Uh-oh, Sam thought, catching Lulu's warily astonished expression. They were headed for meltdown territory.

Wondering if there were any exceptions to be made, Sam tilted his head. "Are they permitted to bring pets into the preschool?" he asked Lulu.

Her cheeks pink with distress, she shrugged. "I don't know. Let me call and ask."

Sam stayed with the kids and got them involved in helping straighten their toys. A few minutes later, Lulu returned. "I spoke with their teacher, Miss Cece. Apparently, it is possible, as long as the pet is up to date on all their vaccinations, is good with kids and the visit is brief."

"How much advance notice do they need?"

"If you've got the right vet records, today is good."

"I do."

Lulu's grin widened. Looking extremely happy they hadn't had to disappoint the boys, she declared, "Well then, kids, looks like your best friend is going to school with you today."

"Yay!" The boys clapped and danced with excitement.

She made another phone call, confirming the visit. Because Beauty was so big and couldn't arrive until midmorning, Sam agreed to follow later and drive his dog separately. Anticipating they might need extra help, Lulu pledged to stay on in the classroom as a volunteer.

When the time came, Sam headed into town. He got there a little early, so he walked Beauty up and down the shady town streets. Pausing to give her water from her travel bowl and making sure she had time to take care of necessities. Finally, Lulu texted that they were ready.

Aware he was almost as excited as the kids, Sam entered the school, stopped by the front office to check in and say hello and then headed back down the hall.

The two-year-olds were buzzing with excitement. Their eyes widened when they saw the extremely gentle brown-and-white dog that stood twice as high as them.

Confessed dog lover Cece Taylor welcomed them into the classroom. The fifty-five-year-old educator directed Sam to take his pet to the open space next to the bulletin board. The rest of the kids sat cross-legged in a semicircle on the carpet.

"Okay, Theo, Andrew, Ethan," Miss Cece said. "Do you boys want to come up here and show us your dog and tell us about her?"

The boys stood importantly. Little chests puffed out, they walked up to Beauty.

"And who is this?" Miss Cece prompted.

"Beauty. Doggy," Theo explained.

"Soft. Pet." Ethan demonstrated how to stroke her fur.

"No ride," Andrew explained gravely, pointing at her back.

Miss Cece flashed an inquisitive look their way.

Sam told the assembled group, "Andrew is telling us we don't ever try to ride the doggy like a horse. Because that's not good. We can pet Beauty, though, because she really likes that."

Enthralled, the kids took this in.

"Are there any questions?" Miss Cece asked.

One of the older little girls in the class raised her hand. When called on, she pointed at Lulu. "Who is that?" she asked.

"And that?" Another child jumped in to point at Sam.

Sam bit down on an oath. A land mine. One that none of the adults in the room had expected. Luckily, the triplets were taking the queries in stride. All three boys grinned proudly.

Theo walked over to Lulu, who was seated on a small chair next to Beauty. He took her face in his hands. Gazed happily into her eyes. "Lulu. *Mommy*," he declared.

Was he calling Lulu Mommy? Sam wondered, barely suppressing a sharp inhalation of surprise and delight.

Andrew walked over to Sam. He motioned for Sam to bend down. When Sam did, Andrew took Sam's face in his hands. "Sam. *Daddy*," he said clearly.

Sam felt himself begin to mist up. He wasn't the only one, either. Lulu's eyes were moist with unshed tears, too.

Ethan walked over to stand between Lulu and Sam. He put one hand on each of them and then walked over to Beauty. He took the big dog's face in his hands. "Family," he said reverently, before taking another big breath and puffing out his little chest.

Andrew and Theo echoed the sentiment. Her lower lip trembling, barely stifling a sob, Lulu flashed a smile as wide as Texas. Tears streaming down her face, she engulfed all three little boys, then Beauty and then Sam, in hug after hug. "That's right, boys, Beauty, Sam and I are all part of your family now," she said huskily.

Not sure when he'd ever felt such joy, Sam swallowed the knot in his throat and embraced them all. The boys had been right. They were a family, and a darned good one. He swallowed around the lump in his throat and held them close.

Hours later, Lulu still felt herself welling up from time to time. To her satisfaction, Sam seemed overwhelmed with happiness, too. In fact, they were brimming with joy as they headed downstairs to finish the dinner dishes.

Lulu picked up where she'd left off an hour earlier. It had become clear their little darlings were in desperate need of their bedtime routine a good forty-five minutes earlier than usual. Which, as it happened, was a good thing, because the cuddling and storybook reading took longer and were rife with more mutual affection than ever.

Sighing contentedly, Lulu began loading the dishwasher. "Whoever said good things come when you least expect them was right."

The fabric of his shirt stretching across his broad shoulders and nicely delineating the muscles in his chest, Sam knelt to pick up green beans and potatoes from the floor. His snug jeans did equally nice things to his lower half.

Gold-flecked eyes twinkling, he slanted her a fond glance. "That was some show-and-tell, wasn't it?" he ruminated softly.

Finished, Lulu wiped down the counters. Sam took out the trash. When he came back, they both stood at the sink and washed their hands. Lulu ripped off a paper towel and handed him one. Now that they finally had a quiet moment alone, she asked what had been nagging at her. "Do you think they were trying to call us Lulu-Mommy and Sam-Daddy, or just explain what our role was in their lives?"

He came closer, gently cupped her face in his large, warm palms. "Both."

Lulu released an uneven breath. "I do love them."

He wrapped his arms around her, inundating her with his steady masculine warmth. "I do, too, sweetheart."

Aware how close she was to falling for him all over

again, she released a reluctant, admiring sigh. "And I think they're beginning to love and trust us."

The question was, when would she and Sam ever love and trust each other as much as they needed to, to have the kind of forever-family she still yearned for? Or would they? Had that window closed? If not for her, for him? And if it had, would it be okay if they were just really great friends and lovers and co-parents to three adorable little boys? Although she knew she was happy as is—wildly happy, in fact—the romantic side of her still wanted more, and that disappointed her. She didn't want to ruin everything by being greedy. They had so very much as it was.

Sam's cell rang. He glanced at the screen. Reluctantly stepped away from her and answered. "Hey, Travis," he said. "Thanks for returning my call."

He had called his attorney? And not mentioned it to her?

Oblivious to her shock, he continued speaking in his husky baritone, "I've got Lulu here with me, too, so I'm going to put you on speakerphone." Sam hit the button and set his cell on the counter in front of them.

Lulu and Travis exchanged greetings. Then Sam said, "We were wondering if there had been news about the background check yet."

Lulu tensed.

Travis replied, "I just talked with the private investigator. He's still tracking something down."

Oh no, Lulu thought.

Sam reached over to take her hand. Gave it a reassuring squeeze. "Any idea what he's looking at?" Sam asked his attorney.

Matter-of-factly, Travis replied, "Liz and I never discuss anything with our clients until we receive the final report. Otherwise, people can get upset for no reason other than records somewhere that weren't complete, or some such."

Sam wrapped his arm around Lulu's shoulders and drew her against his side. "Makes sense," he said. Seeming to understand her silence for the apprehension that it was, he continued, "I'm sure everything will be fine."

Maybe…or maybe not, Lulu thought, worried her and Sam's reckless actions in the past could come back to haunt them now.

"That's our assumption, too," Travis said. "Although…" his voice took on a teasing lilt "…Liz and I did hear what happened in preschool, Lulu-Mommy and Sam-Daddy."

Recalling, Sam and Lulu chuckled in tandem. It was all she could do not to tear up again. "It was definitely a moment," she said proudly.

"A moment that's apparently all over the school," Travis continued. "And since our kids are enrolled there, too, Liz heard about it when she went to pick our girls up. I have to tell you, stuff like that is really going to help your petition to adopt."

"Let's hope so," Lulu said.

It certainly helped her heart.

Hugging her close, Sam drawled, "Speaking of our plans to adopt. Any idea when we *can* expect the report from the investigator?"

"Early next week," his attorney said.

"Okay. Thanks, Travis." Sam ended the call. Satisfaction turned up the corners of his lips. "When we clear that hurdle, we'll be one step closer," he vowed.

Lulu bit her lip, still not so sure. "You really think we're going to be in the clear?" she asked nervously. "That no one will ever know what happened when we were in Tennessee?"

He rocked forward on the toes of his boots. "How could they? For there to be a record of it, there had to be follow-through on our part." His gaze drifted over her. "And we didn't…so there should be absolutely nothing standing in our way."

"And we'll be able to move forward with the adoption! Oh, Sam, it's really going to happen, isn't it?" Lulu threw her arms around his neck. "We're all going to be together! We're going to be a family."

"We really are. In the meantime, I'm thinking I'd like a shower." He fit his lips to hers and kissed her seductively. "Want to join me?"

She splayed her hands across his chest. Felt his heart beat in tandem with hers. "You're serious."

"As can be." He kissed her again, leisurely.

"Then so am I." She kissed him back, then took him by the hand and led him upstairs.

The master bath featured an old claw-foot tub that had been nicely refinished, two sinks and a large modern shower. They stripped down, each helping the other, and climbed in. And although it wasn't the first time they had showered together, it was the first time since they had gotten back together, and definitely the most exciting. Water sluiced down upon them from the rainfall shower fixture above.

They lathered each other from head to toe, taking their time, then stood together under the spray to rinse. Then kissed, fiercely and evocatively, until they were both trembling and groaning for more.

He turned her so she was facing the tile, and he slipped in behind her. One hand explored her breasts, the other moved across her tummy and downward. "So soft and sweet," he murmured against her ear.

She arched her throat, to give him better access. "So hot and hard…"

He laughed and brought her back around to face him. Moved her against the wall. And then they were kissing again, barely stopping to come up for air. Quivering with sensation, she felt her body surrendering all the more.

Sam exited the shower just long enough to get a condom, roll it on. He sank onto the bench built into the shower wall, then pulled her down so she was straddling his lap.

She was wet and open. He seemed intent on giving her what she needed. Kissing her deeply. Finding her with his fingertips, possessing her body and soul, until she felt his desire in every kiss and caress.

He loved her as an equal. As a friend. As a lover, and maybe, just maybe, something more. And she adored him, too. Opening herself up to him in a way she never had before. Celebrating the occasion and possessing him as well, with the tenderness and need and singularity of purpose they both deserved.

Afterward, as they cuddled together in bed, Lulu knew this was what it felt like when it was right, when her life was finally on the brink of being complete.

All she had to do was trust in fate. Trust in Sam. And the love that would bring their new little family together.

Chapter Thirteen

The rest of the week passed blissfully, and on Saturday morning, Sam made his famous blueberry pancakes while they all lounged around in their pajamas. Not surprisingly, the boys picked up on the lack of urgency. As if realizing they would normally be rushing around, looking for shoes and getting dressed, Theo cocked his head. "Me. School?"

Sam knelt down so they were eye to eye. He was still in loose-fitting pajama pants and a short-sleeved gray T-shirt. Thick wheat-colored hair rumpled and standing on end, morning stubble rimming his jaw, he looked slightly on edge. Same as Lulu.

They'd made plans for that afternoon, but this morning it was going to be just the five of them again. That arrangement had not worked out well previously. They were hoping that the boys had been with them long enough that they wouldn't need the distraction of constantly playing with other children to make them happy. That the five of them would be able to feel like the complete family they aspired to be.

Sam smiled down at their little charges. If he was disappointed the boys were already starting to feel restless and on the verge of being unhappy, he did not show it. "Not today, fellas," he said soothingly. "It's Saturday."

Briefly, the boys looked as crestfallen as Sam and Lulu had feared they might be, upon learning there was no school that day. "But we can do other fun things," Sam said cheerfully, rising.

Like what? Lulu wondered. They hadn't discussed this. She moved close enough to feel his body heat. "What did you have in mind?" she asked.

The boys, already bored, wandered back to the play area in the reconfigured family room and began jumping on the sofa.

Keeping one eye on them, to make sure they didn't get too wild, Sam lounged against the counter. "There's a custom backyard play set company over in San Angelo. They've got an air-conditioned sales facility with all the different possibilities set up for kids and their parents to explore. I thought we all might mosey over there and let the boys run around and pick out a swing set for the backyard."

It would sure beat having them jump on and climb all over everything inside the ranch house, Lulu thought. Still… "That sounds like a pretty big investment." Were they getting ahead of themselves? They hadn't even cleared the background check.

Sam glanced over at the boys. They had abandoned the sofa and were now doing somersaults on the rug. He grinned and shook his head in amusement, as the gymnastics turned to a poorly executed game of leapfrog.

He turned back to Lulu. "And a very necessary one, when you think about the fact the closest playground is a good twenty minutes away by car. Convenient to us only when we're already in town."

Winded, the boys collapsed and, lying on their backs, began to talk gibberish among themselves.

Relaxing, Lulu took up a place opposite Sam. She let her gaze drift over the rugged planes of his face. "True."

He looked over at her, as protective as ever. "We're not tempting fate, darlin'." His gaze lingered briefly on her lips before returning to her eyes.

A spiral of heat swept through her, flushing her cheeks. "How did you know that was what I was thinking?" she asked, attempting to keep her mind on the mundane instead of the sizzling chemistry between them.

"That little pleat right here." Sam traced the line between her brows, just above her nose. He caught her around the waist and drew her all the way into his arms. "It always appears when you worry."

Lulu turned her head to check on the boys. Noting they were now calmly playing with their cars and trucks, and that it was safe to give Sam her full attention, she murmured, "I just wish I knew what the PI was still looking into."

"Like Travis said, it's probably nothing to worry about."

She swallowed around the ache in her throat. Aware she thought she'd had it all, one time, only to lose it all, just as swiftly. She released an uneven breath. "But if it is…"

His gaze gentled. "Then we'll fret when the time comes. Right now, we're going to have fun," he promised, a mischievous glint in his eyes. He flattened a soothing palm over her spine. "Otherwise the boys will worry, and we don't want them getting anxious."

She leaned into his reassuring touch, unable to help but think what a good husband and father he would be. "You're right. We don't."

As Sam had predicted, the triplets loved the sales facility. They raced from one sample play yard to another in air-conditioned comfort while Sam and Lulu simultaneously watched over them and checked out the outdoor equipment. The more time went on, the more content she felt.

"You have a beautiful family," the salesman said.

Looking as proud and happy as Lulu felt, Sam wrapped his arm around Lulu's shoulders. Gave her an affectionate squeeze. "We do."

Was this what their weekends would be like when it all did become official? Lulu wondered. Or would they be even better?

She only knew what she hoped.

And what Sam appeared to be counting on, too, she thought, tucking her hand in Sam's.

Together, they went to round up the boys. Eventually, they picked out a sandbox with plenty of room for driving excavators and dump trucks around and an A-frame swing set that held three swings. It came with toddler bucket seats for now, flexible plank-style child seats for later. They agreed that the climbing fort and slide could come later when the boys were big enough to safely handle both.

From there, they went to have dinner with Lulu's brother Matt, and his fiancée, Sara Anderson, and her son.

Although they had napped in the pickup truck, the

boys were tuckered out when they finally arrived home and went through the usual bath time routine.

"Stories!" Theo shouted as they headed for the big leather sofa.

Lulu picked up the stack of favorites, as well as their own homemade book about the changes in the boys' life. With her and Sam sitting cozily side by side and the triplets sprawled across their two laps, they took turns reading through the stack of familiar books. It all felt as comfy and family-oriented as usual, yet when they had finished, the boys looked surprisingly restless. "New. Story," Andrew demanded.

Were they getting bored with the same old tales? Apparently so. Lulu looked at Sam, wanting his input.

"They might have a point," he said, still snuggling close. "Since they do know all the endings."

Aware their bright and lively little boys might need more intellectual stimulation, Lulu suggested, "We could hit the library tomorrow afternoon."

Unfortunately, that did not seem to solve the immediate problem.

Ethan frowned in displeasure. "Story. *Beauty.*"

Not sure what the boys were talking about, although as usual all three seemed to be of the same mind-set, Lulu looked to Sam for help.

Taking her cue, he attempted to clarify. "You want to read a story about a doggy?"

"No. Beauty," Theo insisted vehemently.

"Story. Beauty," Andrew repeated.

Abruptly, it all clicked. "You want us to make our own storybook about Beauty, with pictures of her?" Lulu asked.

"Yay!" the boys shouted in unison.

She and Sam exchanged grins of relief. These were

the kinds of problems they could easily handle. "I think we can do that," she promised. Now that she had experience using the publishing software, it wasn't hard at all.

Pleased their wish was going to be granted, the boys headed to bed. That night, they fell asleep easily.

"I think we're getting a handle on this parenting thing," Lulu mused happily as she and Sam tiptoed from the room.

"I think we're getting a handle on a lot of things," Sam murmured, taking her in his arms and dancing her back toward her bedroom.

Wishing more than ever that the two of them had never called it quits, Lulu asked coyly, "Got something specific in mind, cowboy?"

Lulu was looking at him that way again. The way she once had years ago, every time they were together. The way that said she was his for the taking. But she hadn't been before, and wary of making the same mistake again by assuming too much too soon, he kept to the pace they had agreed upon and the deal they had made.

They were co-parents, first and foremost. Friends. And sometimes lovers.

Although the first time around, they had wanted to get married. Now she saw getting hitched as something to be avoided. He had to remember that.

Take it day by day, moment by moment. Night by night. So he pulled her into his arms. Bent his head to kiss her thoroughly. Showing her all he felt, all they could have, if only she would open up her heart.

Until she moaned deep and low in her throat, arching up against him, and kissed him back with even less restraint than he had shown.

"Beginning to get the idea?" he said. Taking her by the hand, he continued leading her down the hall to her bed.

Eyes glittering with anticipation, she swayed toward him, clearly wanting more. She pressed her lips to his. "Very much so," she whispered.

Prepared to be as relentless as he needed to be in pursuit of her, he drew her flush against him, so she could feel his hardness. He wanted her to know how much she excited him, and he wanted to arouse her, too.

"Because I want you," he ground out against her mouth. "So much…"

She hitched in a breath as they divested each other of their clothes. When they were naked, she murmured, "Oh, Sam, I want you, too…"

He laid her back on the bed, settling between her thighs, sliding lower. Caressing her with the flat of his palms, his fingertips, his lips. Studiously avoiding the part he most wanted to touch. Until she arched and made a soft, helpless sound that sent his desire into overdrive.

She caught his head between her trembling palms. He lifted her against his mouth, circling, retreating, moving up, in. Until at last she fell apart in his arms.

Burning with a need he could no longer deny, he took control of their mesmerizing embrace. Making it as hot and wanton as the kisses she was giving. Finding protection. Lifting and entering her with excruciating slowness and care, making her his in a way that had her surrendering against him. Reveling in the erotic yearning and sweet, hot need. Knowing that this night, this time, she was his, in a way she had never been before. And, if he had his way, always would be.

To Lulu's delight, Sam had plans for their little family Sunday afternoon, as well. Regarding her fondly, he said, "I thought we might drive around the ranch and go see the horses, cattle and cowboys. Then head over to Monroe's Western Wear to get tyke-size cowboy hats and comfy boots and jeans."

"Sounds good to me," she said, returning his affectionate glance. They were feeling more and more like a family with each passing day. So what if they hadn't said they loved each other? She and Sam might not be a traditional couple, but they were a team. And a very good one at that. It was going to have to be enough.

That night, they had dinner with Lulu's brother Cullen, his wife Bridgett and their son Robby. To Lulu's relief, neither her brother nor his new wife inquired into the status of Lulu and Sam's relationship. On the other hand, Beauty, who was back at Hidden Creek and absent from the gathering, was quite the center of focus. The Saint Bernard's name came up a lot while the triplets and eighteen-month-old Robby played with their family dog.

"Beauty. *Play*," Theo explained, petting the top of Riot's head.

"Beauty. *Friend*," Andrew added helpfully.

"Play. *Fun*," Ethan stroked the beagle mix's silky tricolored fur.

In frustration, Theo turned to Sam and Lulu. "Beauty. Here?" he asked.

Abruptly, Lulu realized what the boys were asking, in their abbreviated way.

"I think they want the two of them to meet," Sam said.

Bridgett smiled. "We can probably make that happen."

And that swiftly, a new canine friendship was arranged.

That evening, the boys listened raptly to the new story about Beauty that Lulu and Sam had pulled together the previous night. They were delighted and insisted on hear-

ing it not one but three times before Lulu finally called
a halt.

"More," Andrew demanded earnestly, pointing to the
storybook. *"New."*

His two brothers nodded. "Sam-Daddy," Ethan said,
affectionately patting Sam's chest.

"Lulu-Mommy," Theo added, snuggling close.

"You want us to make a story about us?" Lulu asked.

The boys responded by getting up to give them great
big hugs and smacking kisses. "Yay!" they shouted. More
hugs followed. And then they reared back and said the
words to both of them that Lulu had never expected to
hear, at least not for a very long time.

Wrapping their arms around Lulu's and Sam's necks,
in turn, they chorused, *"Me. Love. Sam-Daddy. Lulu-
Mommy."*

"You can stop crying now," Sam teased two hours
later. He and Lulu were putting the finishing touches on
the story about themselves, complete with pictures from
their current ranches and of themselves and the boys.

"Oh hush, cowboy! You've been welling up all evening, too."

He grinned, guilty as charged. He folded his arms
across his broad chest. Tilting his head, he said thickly,
"It was pretty great, wasn't it? To hear them try to tell
us they loved us?"

Lulu's happiness increased a million fold. "It sure
was."

A brief, contented silence fell. Aware she had never
imagined being so happy, she reached over and took his
hand. "Oh, Sam, I love them so much."

His eyes glistened once again. Using the leverage of

their entwined hands, he brought her closer. "Me, too. More and more each day."

The joyful tears Lulu had been holding back rolled down her cheeks.

"Ah, darlin'." Sam stroked a hand through her hair and pressed a kiss to her temple.

Her spirits soared as he shifted her onto his lap and went about showing her that the affection in the Thompson-Kirkland-McCabe household did not end with the kids and the family's adorable Saint Bernard.

For the first time in a very long time, Lulu felt her life was really and truly complete. Or at least very, very close to being so. Now, if only they'd get the go-ahead from their attorneys, so they could get the adoption process started!

"You want me to drive the kids to school this morning?" Sam asked her the next morning. Since the triplets had adapted to the new routine, it was no longer necessary for both of them to do the drop-off and pickup. They were now alternating.

But the rest of the day, they were still together. Or at least they had been for the last two and a half weeks. Lulu knew that, too, was going to have to end. They both had work responsibilities to honor. Speaking of which... she hadn't been doing as much as she should with hers.

Lulu bit her lip. Sighed. And felt warmth pool through her as she watched Sam's gaze devour her head to toe.

Trying not to think how much she'd like to spend the morning making love with him, Lulu said, "If you don't mind, I'd like to head over to the Honeybee Ranch this morning and tend my remaining hive."

"No problem," he said, his gold-flecked eyes twinkling. Telling herself he couldn't possibly have known what she was wishing, Lulu said goodbye to everyone, made sure the boys had their backpacks and lunches and then headed out herself.

As she drove onto her property, what had once been her sanctuary felt slightly alien. Definitely overly quiet, now that she no longer had honey to sell and customers coming in.

Even her food truck sat idle inside the locked barn.

It was funny, she thought, suiting up and putting on her beekeeper's hat and veil, how much her life had changed since she had first learned about the orphaned boys and began helping Sam care for them. In fact, she was pretty sure it was her most eventful June ever.

Thanks to the help she had received from her beekeeping friends, the bee colony was making progress. The new queen had been accepted by the hive. The brood combs looked healthy. There were adequate honey and pollen stores.

She added water, then replaced the lid on the hive. Picking up her smoker, she headed for the gate. She was just emerging from the mostly empty apiary when Sam's familiar truck drove up.

Alarmed, because he was supposed to be at his ranch checking on things with his crew, she ripped off her hat, veil and gloves and strode toward him. "Everything okay?" she called out.

Sam opened up the door, his cowboy hat slanted sexily across his brow, a fistful of gorgeous flowers in his hand. "It will be," he drawled, heading for her with a seductive grin, "if you'll agree to go on a date with me."

Chapter Fourteen

Sam watched Lulu walk across the lawn toward him, her honey-brown hair cascading over her shoulders. As she got closer, she stepped out of the white bee suit, revealing a pair of thigh-length shorts and a scoop-necked tank that highlighted her stunning curves and long, lissome legs.

Soft lips curving into a smile that spoke volumes about her sassy attitude, she strolled right up to him. Turquoise eyes sparkling, she tossed out, "Hey, cowboy, didn't you know you're supposed to give a gal some notice before you show up, ready to take her out, looking handsome as can be?"

His heart jackhammered in his chest. "You think I'm handsome?" Still clutching the flowers, he flirted shamelessly.

She let out a slow breath that drew his attention to her full shapely breasts. "Oh, yeah." Poking back the brim of an imaginary cowgirl hat, she wickedly looked him up and down.

Figuring he'd kept his distance long enough, he hooked an arm about her waist and tugged her against him. "Nice to hear," he murmured, pressing the bouquet in her hands.

Their fingers brushed as she accepted the first of many gifts he planned to give her. She wrinkled her nose. "Lots of things are nice to hear." She paused. Their eyes met. Emotion shimmered between them. And once again, he was reminded of all the things they didn't yet have.

Like commitment.

Not for the boys. They had that in spades.

But for each other.

He leaned down to kiss her, giving in to instinct and claiming her as his. When the smoldering caress ended, she pulled away, pouting playfully. "You really should have given me notice."

He shrugged, still way too turned on for the beginning of a daytime date. As was she, if the tautness of her nipples was any indication. He rubbed his thumb down the nape of her neck, felt her quiver in response. "Hey, I love you in a bee suit. And out," he couldn't help but tease.

Her eyes sparkled. "I bet." With a frown, she glanced down at her watch. "Seriously, we've only got two hours before pickup."

Taking her by the hand, he led her toward the porch. "Actually, a little more." Wrapping his arm around her waist, he brought her in close to his side. "I called Kelly yesterday and explained that I hadn't had enough time to do the kind of courting I'd like to do and asked if she and Dan would consider taking the kids this afternoon for a playdate."

Lulu chuckled softly. "I am sure it didn't take much coaxing. They're always willing to help romance along..."

Sam nodded. He held the door for her as Lulu moved inside ahead of him. His gaze drifted over the taut, sexy curves of her derriere. "They said yes. Dan's off today. So it won't be a problem to have them all at their place after school."

Lulu led the way into the kitchen. Perspiration dotted her neck, hairline. She set the flowers down on the island, reached into the fridge and brought out two bottles of ice-cold water. "Nice work."

He accepted his with a thanks. Leaning against the counter opposite her, he matched her drink for thirsty drink. "So what did you want to do?"

Grinning, Lulu wiped her damp lips with the back of her hand, let the nearly empty bottle fall to her side. "You really want me to answer that?"

He nodded, serious now. "Yes. I do. You've worked so hard to help make my dreams come true."

She furrowed her brow, looking suddenly wary again. "What kind of dreams?"

"Of having a family," he said casually. *And having you back in my life, to stay*, he wanted to add. Leery she would consider that to be pushing her again, or God forbid, taking her for granted, he went on, "I wanted to say thank you."

Lulu reached for a vase. "You're welcome." Looking abruptly way too serious, she slid the bouquet into the neck and added water. Set it in a prominent place on the kitchen counter.

With a bolstering breath, she turned to him again. "Although I should say thank you, too," she said with the careful politeness usually reserved for strangers, "for welcoming me into your home and making my dreams of family come true, too."

Not sure how his attempt to woo her had gone so awry so fast, Sam forced a smile. Yes, they were great co-parents, lovers and friends, but he wanted more. A *lot* more.

"So…" he said, clearing his throat. "Want to do lunch out?" He cast around for anything that might please her. And get this day date back on track.

To his frustration, she was looking as oddly off-her-game as he was.

"A movie?" he proposed. "Shopping?"

That got her. "Shopping? Come on! You hate shopping!"

Didn't he know it. He shrugged, determined to make this her day. Spreading his hands accommodatingly wide, he flashed her a sexy smile. "Your wish is my command today."

Her cheeks lit up with a rosy blush.

He had the feeling she was about to tell him she wanted to make love. But before she could utter another word, her cell phone chimed at the exact same time as his. Lulu started, recalling as swiftly as Sam the last time that had happened. Alarmed, she said, "I hope it's not the school."

It was not.

It was their attorneys.

Lulu knew by what Liz and Travis would not say to them on the phone that their worst fears were being realized, so she went upstairs to hurriedly shower and change into business casual clothes. Then she and Sam drove into town.

Liz and Travis were waiting for them in the conference room. "Why don't you both have a seat?" Liz said.

Sam held Lulu's chair for her, then sat down beside her. As usual, he wasted no time cutting to the chase. "You found something problematic, didn't you?"

Travis grimaced. "Definitely something interesting."

"The two of you are still married," Liz said.

"Still?" Lulu croaked.

Sam asked, "What are you talking about?"

"More to the point, how do you know this?" Lulu demanded, the news hitting her like a gut punch.

Travis looked down at the papers in front of him. "Official state records show you eloped in the Double Knot Wedding Chapel in Memphis, Tennessee, on Monday, March 14, over ten years ago. Alongside another couple, Peter and Theresa Thompson, in a double wedding ceremony."

Lulu gulped. "But our union was never legal," she pointed out, trying to stay calm while Sam sat beside her in stoic silence.

Liz countered, "Ah, actually, it is legal. In fact, it's still valid to this day."

Sam reached over and took her hand in his, much as he had the first time they had been in this room together. "How is that possible?" Lulu asked weakly.

"We never mailed in the certificate of marriage, or the license, to the state of Tennessee," Sam said.

"And for our union to be recorded and legal, we would have had to have done that," Lulu reiterated.

"Well, apparently, the owners of the Double Knot Wedding Chapel did, and your marriage was recorded," Travis said. "And is still valid to this day, near as we can tell. Unless you two got a divorce or an annulment somewhere else? Say, another country?"

"Why would we do that? We didn't know we were married," Sam returned.

Lulu noted her "husband" did not appear anywhere near as upset as she was. She forced herself to settle down. With a dismissive wave of her hand, she told everyone in the room, "It doesn't matter. We'll just explain we were too young, or at least at nineteen I was too young to know what I was doing," she amended hastily, "and get an annulment now."

Again, Liz shook her head. "Sorry. It's been too long. It would have to be a divorce."

Lulu groaned. Talk about a day going all wrong! First, Sam had completely knocked her off guard by impulsively asking her out on a date. And now this! She twisted her hands and asked, "Is it possible we could obtain a divorce, without anyone finding out?"

"You mean like social services or the court?" Travis asked. "No."

Beside her, Sam went into all-business mode. "How does this development affect our proposed petition to adopt?"

Lulu noticed he hadn't said *mistake*.

Liz tapped her pen against the table. "It certainly makes it a great deal more complicated."

Lulu tried to get a grip and adopted Sam's no-nonsense tone. "In what sense?" she asked.

Travis sat back in his chair. "To become guardians, the bar is not that high, if the parents named you in their will. Mostly because guardianship can be terminated rather easily, for any number of reasons. However, adoption is permanent and cannot easily be undone." He cleared his throat. "So when it comes to that process of qualifying, social services and the courts want to see a stable, loving environment for the children. Anything that points to the opposite, like your secret elopement, equally impulsive breakup, and the fact you did not properly follow-through with either an annulment or a divorce and had no idea you were still married, can send up a red flag."

Lulu gulped. "How do we fix this?"

"You could admit you made a mistake, get an amicable divorce and prove you can get along in the aftermath."

Frowning, Sam asked, "How long would all that take?"

Travis made a seesawing gesture. "Potentially months, if not years, to satisfy the court."

Sam leaned forward, gaze narrowing. "And if we stay married, then what kind of detrimental impact will it have on our proposal to adopt?"

"Less of one. But," Liz said firmly, "if you two choose to go that route, you have to show real commitment to each other, as well as the children."

Lulu's anxiety rose. More and more this seemed like an impossible predicament. "How do we do that?" she asked.

Their lawyers exchanged telltale glances, then shrugged. "That is up to the two of you."

At Sam's suggestion, he and Lulu picked up some sandwiches and coffees from the bistro in town, and then retreated to Lulu's ranch to come up with a strategy for dealing with the marital crisis they suddenly found themselves in.

"I can't believe it," Lulu said miserably, burying her face in her hands.

Sam could. He'd always felt married to Lulu in his heart, ever since they said their vows. It was what had made it so hard for him to move on. What Lulu was feeling, though, he had no clue.

"Can't?" he asked before he could stop himself, realizing he had to know where he stood with her. "Or *don't* want to believe it?"

She jumped out of her seat and whirled to face him. Hands on her hips. Like him, she'd barely touched her food. "Would you please stop doing that?" she asked with icy disdain.

The resentment he'd stuffed deep inside rose to the surface. "Stop doing what?" *Wanting you?*

She winced. Looking guilty as all get-out, which of course, she should, since it was her abrupt change of heart, not his, that had ultimately put them in this mess.

She huffed in answer to his question. "Stop bringing up all the angst we felt back then!"

"Can't help it." Within him, anger and irritation surged. "It was a lousy thing to do, insist we get married, along with our friends. And then," he continued, the words coming out along with the hurt, "four days later, tell me the only way we could continue as husband and wife was if we kept it a secret!"

She took another deep breath, suddenly appearing oddly vulnerable. "I wasn't saying permanently!" She gestured broadly, then started to pivot away from him.

Not about to let her run away from him again, he stopped her with a light hand to her shoulder. Turned her slowly back to face him. And finally asked what he'd wanted to know for years. "Why say it at all?"

An emotional silence stretched between them.

He let his hand fall to his side. "You either loved me or you didn't, and apparently you didn't."

"It's more complicated than that, and you know it."

A muscle ticked in his jaw. "Then why, Lulu?" He gritted out. "Why did you run scared?"

Another long, awkward silence fell. "My parents would not have understood."

Aggravated to find her still using that lame excuse, he gave her a chastising glance. "There's no way to know that, because we never gave them a chance to support us."

"It's not like you told anyone in your family!" Lulu

said, just as bitterly. Reminding him she wasn't the only one who had suffered from a hefty dose of pride. She stepped forward and jabbed an accusing finger at his chest. "Since you said we'd either go public with our marriage immediately, or it was all over. And no one would ever have to know!"

Seeing she was about to bolt again, he let out a rough breath and stepped closer. "Can you blame me?"

She tossed her head, silky hair flying in every direction. "For having a 'my way or the highway' approach?" she shot back. "Yes, I can, since marriage is supposed to be a fair and equal partnership."

Her words hit their target. She had a point. He shouldn't be lashing out. He shook his head. "I'm sorry," he said guiltily. "I'm upset." They had been so close to having everything they wanted. And now...

Lulu released a deep breath and grew quiet once again. "We're both upset, Sam." She shoved her hair away from her face. Shook her head in misery. "The big issue is where do we go from here?"

That, at least, was easy, Sam thought. "Isn't it obvious? We stay married."

Lulu's day went from bad to worse in sixty seconds. She stared at the handsome cowboy opposite her, wondering how she had ever imagined the two of them were living in some sort of fairy tale. "Are you serious?"

Looking more resolute than ever, he replied, "We want to adopt the kids. Our best shot at doing that is by being married. And since we already are, why not just leave it as is and go forward as husband and wife?"

How about because we don't love each other? Lulu thought. But not about to reveal the direction of her thoughts, she countered sarcastically, "Just like that?

Presto, change-o, snap our fingers, and we're a happily married couple?"

Even though, if she were honest, she would have to admit that lately she had been feeling as if they were on the verge of being just that.

"Why not? We're already spending time together every day. Sleeping together. Raising three kids together and living under the same roof. Why not just admit that staying married is the best avenue for raising the kids and making them feel safe and secure and loved?"

Because, Lulu thought, *if I do that, then I'm one step away from opening up my heart and admitting the real reason why I've never really been able to get serious about anyone else but you, Sam*. "Because we'd have to tell everyone what we did back then," she blurted out.

Again, he clearly did not see what the problem was. "So?" His gruff response was a direct hit to her carefully constructed defenses.

"It's embarrassing," she whispered, the heat moving from her chest into her face. She threw up her hands and paced. "It makes us look idiotic and reckless."

Sam crossed his arms. Determined, it seemed, to win this argument. His gaze sifted over her before returning ever so slowly to her eyes. "Or wildly in love. I mean, isn't that why people usually elope?"

"Except we weren't wildly in love, Sam." If they had been, they never would have split up and stayed apart for almost a decade. Would they?

He sobered, looking pensive. "Well, what do you want to do, Lulu?" he asked in exasperation. "Split up again and go through the hell of divorce, because even an uncontested one is just that, and then try to adopt?"

Put that way, it did sound unreasonable.

"And what if getting divorced not only ruins our

chances of ever adopting the triplets," he said, in an increasingly rusty voice, "but also casts a bad light on our character and gets them removed from our guardianship, too?"

Lulu swallowed around the lump in her throat. "I couldn't bear that." The thought of losing the triplets was on par with how she had felt losing Sam. Heartbreakingly awful.

Sam compressed his lips. "Well, neither could I."

A stony silence fell.

Lulu weighed the possibilities. Life with Sam and the kids. Life without. There really was no other choice. Not if they didn't want to disappoint literally everyone. "So we're in agreement," she said, trying not to cry. She swallowed hard, aware she had never felt so trapped or miserable. She lifted her gaze to his. "We bite the bullet and stay married for the sake of the kids."

Sam locked eyes with her, looking no happier than she felt. He exhaled grimly, ran a hand through his hair. "I really don't see any other way out of this. Do you?"

Chapter Fifteen

Unfortunately, Lulu did not see any other way out. So they asked Dan and Kelly to keep the kids a little longer and went to see her parents first, figuring they could then leave it to Rachel and Frank to spread the word.

As they sat down together at the kitchen table, Lulu said, "Y'all remember spring break, my sophomore year of college, when I went on a country music tour with some of my best girlfriends?"

Her parents nodded, perplexed, unable to see where this was going.

Hating to disappoint them, Lulu knotted her hands in front of her. "Well, I lied to you," she admitted shamefully. "I *was* in Tennessee. But I was staying with Sam that week, not a group of girls."

Her parents looked at Sam. "I apologize for that," he said with gruff sincerity. "We should have told you the truth."

Her parents paused. "I assume there is a reason you're telling us all this now?" her father said.

Lulu nodded. "There is." She explained how she and Sam had accompanied their friends Peter and Theresa to Tennessee to be the witnesses for their secret wedding ceremony.

Sam reached over and took her hand. Buoyed by the warmth and security of his touch, she plunged on, "I was so caught up in the romance of it all—" *and my incredible, overwhelming feelings for Sam*, she added silently "—that I suggested we make it a double wedding."

Sam lifted a hand. "For the record, I was all too ready to jump in."

"So we eloped, too," Lulu confessed. "And for the rest of our spring break," she admitted wistfully as Sam's hand tightened over hers, "everything was wonderful." For a few heady days, she'd felt all her dreams had come true.

"What happened to change all that?" her dad asked. "And make you break up?"

"When it came time to go home, the reality of what we had done set in for me." Hard.

The memory of that last horrible fight was not a good one. Sam withdrew his hand, sat back.

Tears blurred her vision once again. Embarrassed, she continued, "I knew we'd acted recklessly and I was afraid to tell anyone else what we'd done. And I especially didn't want to disappoint the two of you." Unable to look her "husband" in the eye, she related sadly, "Sam refused to live our marriage in the shadows, so we broke up."

"And got the marriage annulled?" her mother assumed.

"Actually…" Sam went on to explain the confusion

over the paperwork that had followed. "We just found out we're still legally married."

Her parents took a moment to absorb that information. "Which puts us in a little bit of a quandary," Lulu said.

"Little?" her father echoed, finally appearing as upset with her as Lulu had initially expected him to be.

"Okay. It's a pretty big problem," she conceded, chagrined. "But Sam and I are going to figure this out."

"Well." Her mother sighed. "First, I wish you had come to us at the time and told us what was going on, so we could have made sure there were no lingering legal snafus. And supported you. And we *would* have supported you, Lulu, no matter what you thought then. Or think now…"

Her dad, calming down, nodded.

"Second," Rachel said, with a gentle firmness, "as for you being fearful of our opinion, when it comes to your life—" she paused to look long and hard at the two of them "—it only matters what *you* two feel in *your* hearts, not what anyone else thinks." She reached across the table to take Lulu's and Sam's hands. Squeezed. "Furthermore, your family will defend your right to make those choices for yourself, by yourselves, even when we don't approve or understand them."

Her dad covered their enjoined hands with his own. "Your mother and brothers and I want you to be happy, sweetheart. And the same goes for you, Sam." He regarded them both with respect.

"It's up to you to figure out what will make you feel that way and then go for it," Rachel added gently.

Everyone disengaged hands. Another silence fell, even more awkward and fraught with untenable emotions.

"Do you know what you're going to do?" her mom asked finally.

Lulu and Sam looked at each other. "Stay married," they answered in unison.

Sam draped his arm across the back of Lulu's chair and continued with the same steady affability that made him such a good leader. "We think it would provide a more stable environment for the kids."

Frank pushed back his chair and got up to make coffee. Once again, he seemed loaded for bear. "You really think you can make an arrangement like this work?"

Lulu didn't see any choice if they wanted to help the kids. But sensing it would be a mistake to tell her parents that, she answered, "Yes." She hauled in another breath, admitting a little more happily, "Sam and I have recently gotten back together, anyway, so it just makes sense for us to stay married and build on that."

Beside her, Sam seemed calm and accepting of the predicament they found themselves in. Her parents regarded them with equal parts doubt and consideration. Which amped up her own wariness. But to her surprise, Frank and Rachel didn't try to talk them out of it.

"Okay, then," her mom said finally. "But if you're going to stay married—" her regard was stern, unrelenting "—your dad and I want you to be as serious as the institution of marriage requires this time. And do it right by officially and publicly recommitting to each other and saying your vows before all your family and friends. That way, everyone—including and especially the two of you—will know it is not just a whim that can be easily discarded. But an honorable, heartfelt promise you can both be proud of."

"I don't see why you're so upset," Sam said, late into the following week.

Lulu pushed away from her laptop, where she had

been dutifully compiling the expected guest lists for her parents. "Because it's all so unnecessary!" she fumed, stepping out back where the newly installed swings and sandbox sat in the warmth of a perfect summer night.

With the triplets soundly asleep and now snoozing happily through most nights, she should be relaxing and getting to know Sam again. Instead, she was slaving away on the endless To Do lists her parents kept giving her.

She swung around to face Sam, her shoulder knocking into his. "I don't see why we even have to have a wedding, when everyone in the whole county—heck, probably the whole state, thanks to the McCabe-Laramie grapevine!—knows our story."

He reached out to steady her, then lounged beside her against the deck railing. His hands braced on either side of him, he continued to study her face, his expression as inscrutable as his mood the last few days.

Unable to quell the emotions riding roughshod inside her, she challenged softly, "Why do we have to go through the motions of getting married again?" If he'd just told her parents no…

He leaned toward her earnestly. "Because the kids deserve it," he returned with a chivalry that grated on her nerves even more than his calculated calm.

The heat of indignation climbed from her chest, into her face. "They're not old enough to realize—"

"But they will be one day," he countered. "Do we really want them to have to weather not just the tragic loss of their parents and the chaos that ensued regarding their guardianship, but a scandal regarding their adoptive parents, too?"

She curled her hands over his biceps, finding much needed solace in his masculine warmth. "It's not like getting married all over again erases the elopement and paperwork snafu that followed."

He wrapped both arms about her waist. "But it brings closure and a well-respected, time-honored path to the future stability of our family." Tugging her closer still, he reached up to tuck a strand of hair behind her ear. "And proving we are serious about staying together," he continued tenderly, "not just as co-guardians or lovers and friends but as husband and wife, *will* bolster our efforts to adopt."

Abruptly feeling as trapped as she had during their conversation with her parents, she pivoted away and stepped farther into the warm and breezy summer night. Stars sparkled in the black velvet sky overhead. A quarter moon shone bright. "That's assuming we *can* still adopt after all this."

He clamped his lips together, as if he was not going to continue, then did, anyway. "You heard what Liz and Travis said about this." He followed her down into the grass. "We will be able to, we're just going to have to wait a little while and prove we have a solid relationship before submitting our application."

Lulu breathed in the minty scent of his breath. "I get all that," she said grumpily.

His eyes tracked her as she paced restlessly back and forth. "But…?"

She came closer and tipped her chin up at him. "I just don't see why I have to have a wedding dress and a whole big reception complete with a live band and a harpist and a flute and five attendants, when we could just as easily say our I dos in jeans and T-shirts."

He gave her a quelling look. "You really want to give people the impression that this means so little to us we couldn't even bother to get properly dressed?"

Okay, so maybe she was taking her resistance to all the hoopla too far.

"Your attendants are all family, and your sisters-in-laws and your brothers all want to participate in this day. So why not let them be members of the wedding party? Plus, as your mom has pointed out on *numerous* occasions for the last several weeks, you are their *only* daughter. They want the privilege and pleasure of seeing you get married on the ranch, the way you all used to envision, when you were growing up."

Damn, why did he have to be so reasonable when making his points?

Recalling how much she hated arguing with him and coming out the loser, she steered the conversation in another direction. "Your family isn't making such a fuss."

His stoicism took on a tinge of sadness. "That's because we're all scattered all over the world now, since all five of my sisters opted for demanding international jobs. And none of them can get here till the very last moment."

Lulu sensed there was more. "And…?" she prodded gently.

One corner of his lips turned down. "No one's actually said it, but I think it's hard for them, having the first wedding, without either of my parents still here with us on earth."

Lulu drew in a breath, guilt washing over her. She hadn't meant to be so insensitive. "Oh, Sam. I'm so sorry about that."

"It's okay." He squared his broad shoulders, dealing with trouble the way he always did. Head-on. He flashed her a grin. "I think they're still looking down on us from up above. And what they are telling us, Lulu…is that you need to get yourself in gear."

Lulu knew Sam was right.

So she tried.

She went to her final dress fitting. Approved the tuxes Sam had picked out for him and the boys. Went with Sam to taste wedding cake and pick out a band. And sat down with the florist.

But when it came to the last and final thing, she balked.

"I don't want to be married by a minister or say traditional wedding vows."

Sam gave her the long-suffering look that had become way too commonplace during the weeks of wedding prep. He continued getting ready for bed. "How come?"

Because this all still felt like a travesty. Like the romance and the enthralling passion was gone, and now all they had left was the duty of recommitment.

Leery of admitting that out loud, though, for fear of hurting his feelings, Lulu washed off her makeup. "I'd prefer a justice of the peace."

Sam stripped down to his boxers and a T-shirt, then walked into the bathroom. "And why's that?"

Trying not to notice how buff he looked or how much she always seemed to want to make love to him, Lulu layered toothpaste onto her brush. "Because when we got married before, we were too young to know what we were doing."

"And now it's different?" he prompted.

"Yes, totally different. Now that we're old enough to know what we are doing, we are going in with clearer heads and are on the same page about the fact that our nuptials aren't romantically or spiritually motivated." She lounged against the marble counter. "Rather, it's just more of a…an optimal agreement about how we're going to live in the future. So." She drew in a deep breath. "That being the case, it seems like we should use a justice of the peace instead of a minister."

That look again. A very long exhalation. Another heartfelt pause.

"Okay," he said finally. "A justice of the peace it is. What do you want to do about the vows?"

Lulu brushed her teeth, rinsed, spit. As did he. "Maybe we could each write our own."

She expected an argument. Instead, he set his toothbrush back in the holder next to hers and said, "That'll work."

Aware all over again how cozy and right it felt to share space with him like this, Lulu said, "You don't mind?"

"Not at all." Coming close enough to take her in his arms, he gazed down at her lovingly and sifted his hand through her hair. "In fact, I kind of like the idea."

As it turned out, however, Lulu did not enjoy writing her vows to Sam any more than she had liked any of the other wedding preparations. Mostly because she could not figure out what to say. Reciting poetry just wasn't *them*. Everything she wrote sounded either disingenuous or lame. Or both.

Finally, there were just three days left before the big event. And she was nowhere close to having anything to say.

She moaned over her laptop, where she had been continuously typing...and deleting...and typing...and deleting.

Sam sank down on the big leather sofa next to her. With the kids and Beauty asleep upstairs in the nursery, the house was oddly quiet. He draped his arm around her shoulders. "What's wrong, sweetheart?"

Aware this part of her life felt more out of control than ever, Lulu buried her face in her hands. "I'm never going to get my vows written."

Settling closer, he gave her an encouraging squeeze. "Do you want my help?"

Briefly, she turned her head and rested her face against his shoulder. She loved snuggling up to him, especially when her emotions were in turmoil. He made her feel so protected. "No." She sighed. "It has to come from me."

Looking devilishly handsome with the hint of evening beard rimming his face, he bussed the top of her head. "Give it time. It'll come."

Would it? "What if it doesn't?" Lulu lamented, her mood growing ever more troubled. She looked deep into Sam's eyes. "What then?"

They had been down this road before, Sam thought, at the end of their passion-filled Tennessee honeymoon. Then, it had been post-wedding jitters. Was this the pre-wedding jitters?

He hadn't talked her out of making a mistake the last time and heartbreak had ensued. He wouldn't let her run away again.

Tilting her face toward his, he gently stroked her cheek. "There is no rule that says we have to write our own vows, Lulu. We can just go back to the tried and true." Which would be a heck of a lot easier, since he hadn't written his vows yet, either. Although he wasn't stressing out about it.

Lulu shot to her feet. Her eyes were steady but her lower lip trembled. "I can't stand up in front of everyone we love and say traditional vows, Sam."

He rose, too. "Why not?"

Regret glimmered briefly in her gaze. She seemed to think she had failed on some level. "Because they're not true!"

He stepped closer and took her rigid body in his arms. "You'd leave me if I was sick? Or poor?"

She lifted her chin and speared him with an outraged look. "No, of course not," she conceded.

"You don't plan to take me as your lawfully wedded husband?" he asked, his own temper beginning to flare.

As she spoke, her face grew pale, her shoulders even stiffer. She shook her head, determined, it seemed, to think the worst of them. "We're already legally hitched."

He stared at her in frustration. "You don't want to love and cherish me?"

"I…" She sent him a confused glance, making no effort at all to hide her reluctance to further their romance. "You mean love like a friend?" she asked warily.

His heart rate accelerated. "Like a wife loves a husband."

She swallowed, looking miserable all over again. Shoving a hand through her hair, she paced away from him. "See? This is why I don't like this!"

"You've lost me, darlin'." He followed her over to the fireplace. "Don't like what?"

She spun around to face him, the soft swell of her breasts lifting and lowering with every anxious breath she took. "Having to analyze our relationship and spell everything out."

These were not the words of a bride who was blissfully in love. These were the words of a woman who was desperately trying to find a way out of getting hitched. He positioned himself so she had no choice but to look at him. "Our relationship won't stand the test of time, is that what you're saying?"

"Of course we'll be together for the kids' sake. For as long as they need us," she said, her eyes glittering. "But we don't have to go through all this rigmarole to do that,

Sam. We could just continue on, as we have been, as we would have, had we not become aware we were still legally married."

Sam forced himself to show no reaction. He might not want to hear this but he had half expected her to say something similar. "You're saying you want a divorce?"

"No!" Still holding his eyes—even more reluctantly now, he noticed—she gulped. "I'm saying I don't want to go through with this wedding." Tears blurred her eyes, and her lower lip trembled all the more. "If they need us to restate our vows, and honestly I don't see why in the world we need to go to the trouble to do that since our marriage is legal just as it is, then I'd rather just elope again. And make the statement that way."

Sam stood, arms crossed. "Thereby proving what, exactly, Lulu? That we're still the impulsive idiots we were before?"

Huffing out a breath, she went back to her laptop and closed it with more care than necessary. "No," she said. She slid her computer back into its case, zipped it shut. "We would be doing what other couples do when they decide the hoopla is all too much and that life has gotten too crazy. They run off and elope."

He took her by the shoulders and held her in front of him. "We did that, Lulu. It didn't work out so well."

Case held against her chest, she eased away. "I was a lot younger." She stalked into the kitchen.

He watched her set the case down. "True. But still just as skittish when it comes to making an actual commitment."

She opened the fridge. "I'm *completely* committed to the children."

"Just not to me."

She spun back to face him, a riot of color filling her cheeks. "Please don't misinterpret this."

He reached past her to get a beer for himself. His gut tightened as he twisted off the cap. "What other way is there to interpret it, darlin'? You want to stay married to me, so long as you don't have to publicly act like you mean it."

She took a sip of water. He took a swig of beer.

"I'm *living here*, aren't I?"

He grimaced. "As a matter of convenience."

Her gaze narrowing, she set her bottle down with a thud. "Well, that makes sense, because you invited me to *bunk here* as a matter of convenience."

An accusatory silence fell.

She came nearer, her hurt obvious. "I don't understand why you're so upset with me. For once in my life, I don't care what people think about this situation we've found ourselves in. I don't care if my parents are going to be disappointed or mad at me."

There was a time when that would have pleased him immensely, to know that she put their relationship above all else. Now, it felt like a booby prize.

"I only care what *we* think and feel is right for us."

He tore his eyes away from the way her knee-length shorts hugged her hips, her cotton T-shirt her breasts. "Which would be…?"

Noticing her hair was falling out of the clip, she undid the clasp and let her mane fall across her shoulders. "To just skip this whole travesty of a wedding and leave things as is."

"Meaning married."

"Technically." She ran her fingers through the silky strands, pushing them into place, then leaned against the opposite counter, her hands braced on either side of her. "And living together."

He definitely felt burned by her casual attitude. "As co-parents."

"Yes." She caught his hand. "Don't you see, Sam? Everything was great until we found we were still legally hitched."

It had been—and it hadn't. The feel of her smooth fingers in his brought only partial comfort. He tried and failed to summon up what little gallantry he had left. "Just like it was great when we were on a honeymoon." A muscle ticked in his jaw. "But then when we had to go home and tell our families what we had done, it was not so great."

She flushed and shook her head in silent remonstration. "There's no comparison between then and now, Sam," she warned.

"Isn't there?" he asked bitterly. Their glances meshed, held. "You're doing exactly what you did before."

She looked at him, incredulous.

"Recklessly jump all in with me—all the while swearing your devotion—only to jump all out."

Her eyes shone even as her low tone took on a defiant edge. "I won't leave the kids, Sam, if that's what you're worried about."

He knew that. Was even grateful for it.

"But you would be right back out that door if the kids weren't here," he countered, before he could stop himself. "Wouldn't you?"

She stared at him, as if feeling every bit as boxed in— and deeply disappointed—as he felt. Like they needed to take a step back. Give each other time to breathe. Figure out what they really felt. "I don't know how to answer that," she said finally, her chin quivering.

"Sadly, I do." He paused to give her a slow, critical once-over. Wondering all the while how they ever could have deluded themselves into thinking this would work. "We never should have told your parents we would renew our vows. Or fooled ourselves into thinking we could carry off this charade," he said, pain knotting his gut. "And this is what any marriage between us is to you, isn't it, Lulu? A charade?"

Her disillusionment grew. "Given the way this wedding has come about, how could it be anything but?" she asked, her face a polite, bland mask.

She moved closer still, imploring now. "Which is why I can't seem to write my vows no matter how hard I try." She lifted her chin. In control, again. "And why we should cancel it, Sam. So we can go back to the way things were before marriage entered the mix."

It wasn't the legality of the situation that was destroying them. It was her refusal to open up her heart. "I asked you this before but I am going to ask you again. And this time, I want an honest answer." He propped his hands on her shoulders and bore his eyes into hers. "You want a divorce?"

She flinched. "No, of course I don't want a divorce now!"

Now...

Which meant...

Releasing her, his feelings for her erupted in a storm of anger and sorrow. "But you will, won't you?" he concluded bitterly, wishing like hell he had seen this coming. Like their second time around would end any other way. "Maybe not tomorrow. Or the next. But one day..."

She compressed her lips. "You're twisting everything I've said."

He told himself he was immune to her hurt. He had to be. For everyone's sake, one of them needed to be reasonable. "Well, one thing is clear. For us, marriage is and always has been a mistake. We can be co-parents, Lulu, but that is all."

She blinked. "*You're* throwing down the gauntlet and issuing an ultimatum to me? *Again?*"

Not happily.

He shook his head, and with a heavy sigh, said, "No. I'm doing what you've been trying to do, indirectly, for weeks now, Lulu. I'm calling an end to our romantic relationship. This time, for good." Heart aching, he stormed out.

Chapter Sixteen

With a heavy heart, Lulu went to see her parents at their ranch. They took one look at her face and sat her down with them at the kitchen table. "Tell us what's going on," her mom urged gently while her father made them all a pot of coffee.

Pushing away the dreams of what might have been, Lulu knotted her hands in front of her. "Sam and I are still planning to adopt the kids together, but we're not going to have a wedding on Saturday afternoon after all." Lulu swallowed around the lump in her throat. "So it would help me out a lot," she continued, swiping at a tear slipping down her cheek, "if you could help me notify everyone."

"Of course we'll help out, honey." Her dad got out the cream and sugar. Added three mugs to the table. "But…?" He looked at her mom, with the same kind of parental telepathy she and Sam had been sharing.

"...are you sure?" Rachel interjected, handing her a box of tissues.

Wiping away a fresh onslaught of tears, Lulu forced herself to be honest. "I really thought I could do it." Her heart aching, she paused to look her folks in the eye. "Build on everything I feel for Sam and the kids and marry him strictly as a matter of convenience. But—" she felt the hot sting of shame that she ever could have been so shortsighted "—when we started trying to work on our vows, I realized there was no way we could really do this without it all being a lie. And I couldn't base our entire relationship on that. Never mind pretend," she continued thickly, "in front of everyone that it was going to be a real marriage." Her voice trembled. "When I knew in my heart it was all a sham."

"And Sam thinks it's a sham, too?" Her dad brought the carafe over to the table and poured coffee into mugs. Not surprisingly, he was more focused on fixing this problem than consoling her.

Aware she hadn't a clue what Sam was thinking or feeling, Lulu stuttered, "I...ah..."

"Did he actually *say* that it was untruthful for him, too?" her attorney-mom asked, in her cross-examination voice.

"No," Lulu admitted miserably.

"Then what *did* he say?" Rachel persisted.

Sam's angry words still reverberating in her mind, Lulu admitted grimly, "That if I couldn't find some wedding vows that would work for us and go through with the wedding on Saturday, our romantic relationship was off. Permanently this time."

Her dad shook his head in mute remonstration, for once not taking her side. "Honestly, Lulu. Can you blame the guy?"

"Hey!" Lulu scowled, feeling indignant. To calm herself, she stirred cream and sugar into her coffee and lifted the mug to her lips, breathing in the fragrant steam. "He never once said he loved me. Not this time around, anyway…!" So what choice had she had, no matter what her feelings were? A fraud was a fraud! And that was no example to set for the kids, never mind a foundation to base a marriage on.

"So." Her mother sighed in regret. "You don't trust the two of you to be able to sustain a romantic relationship that will go the distance."

Softly, Lulu admitted this was so.

Her mom studied her over the rim of her mug. "Will you be able to be friends?"

Lulu took another sip, and finally said, albeit a little uneasily, "When the dust clears, I think so."

Her dad sat down beside her mom. "What about the children?" he asked.

"We still plan to adopt them."

"Together?" he questioned.

"Yes."

"Living separately," he continued to press, "or under one roof?"

Lulu flushed. Aware that hadn't been completely worked out, but she could assume. "Under one roof, just the way we have been."

Her mom picked up where her dad left off. "And you have faith this arrangement will work."

Lulu replied without hesitation. "Yes."

Rachel's eyes narrowed. "Why?"

Lulu struggled to find the words that would explain what she knew in the deepest recesses of her soul to be true. She looked both her parents in the eye. "Because that part of our life together just works and works really well. And we never ever disappoint each other in that regard."

Her mom's brow furrowed. "And you think not disappointing each other is key?"

Lulu lifted a hand. "Of course."

"Oh, honey," Rachel said, getting up to engulf Lulu in a hug. Her dad came around the other side and joined in. "Disappointment is part of life."

They drew back to face her once again. "The more you love someone, the more likely it is that you will disappoint each other from time to time," her dad said gently but firmly.

Her mom nodded. "It's those highs and lows and the ability to weather each storm and come back even stronger, as a couple and a family, that make loving worthwhile."

Thursday morning, Sam had just dropped the kids off at preschool and returned to his ranch, when a caravan of five pickup trucks and SUVs came up the lane.

All five of Lulu's brothers got out and walked toward him. None looked the least bit happy.

Sam bit down on an oath. Great. This was all he needed after the week he'd had. With him and Lulu more or less alternating care of the kids when possible, and doing the polite-strangers dance around each other when it wasn't.

Thus far, they'd manage to keep the boys from picking up on the breech between them, but whenever he and Lulu faced off alone, even for a few minutes, the residual hurt and anger was palpable. To the point they'd more or less taken to completely avoiding each other.

"Told you that you'd be seeing us if you hurt our sister again," Dan drawled.

This would be comical if he hadn't spent the entire night nursing a broken heart.

"I didn't hurt her." Sam pushed the words through his teeth.

Dan adopted a law officer's stance. "Then why is she over at Mom and Dad's ranch, crying her heart out over a potentially canceled wedding?"

Potentially?

Did that mean Lulu was having second thoughts about calling their love affair quits, too? Or just that her folks weren't willing to let her off the hook?

There was no way to tell without speaking to Lulu about it in person.

Sam glared back at the McCabe posse. He curtailed the urge to put his fist through something, anything. "You'll have to ask her that, since she's the one who found it impossible to stand up in front of family and friends and say I do."

"Then what was she going to say?"

"That was the problem. She couldn't figure it out. And was apparently tired of trying."

A contemplative silence fell among the six men.

Chase squinted, his calm, analytical CEO temperament coming to the fore. "I can't believe she would react that way without a very good reason."

Well, she had, Sam thought grimly.

"What aren't either of you telling us?"

A lot of things actually. Like the fact I opened up my heart and soul to her and it still wasn't enough. Or the fact I still don't want a divorce, even though Lulu all but came out and admitted in a roundabout way that her only attraction to me is physical.

Looking very much like the chivalrous ex-soldier he was, Matt rubbed the flat of his hand beneath his jaw. "Are you protecting her?"

Yes, Sam thought, *I am*. Which on the surface wasn't

surprising. Like the McCabes, he had been raised to be a Texas gentleman, too. And gentlemen didn't tell a woman's secrets.

Ever. But this went deeper than that. For the first time, he found himself caring about what people thought. Not about him. But about Lulu. He didn't want anyone thinking less of her because of mistakes they'd both made. So he remained mum.

Jack analyzed the situation with a physician's empathy. "One thing's clear. You're both miserable."

Sam tried not to hang any hope on that. "That's kind of hard to believe since she's been dragging her heels," he scoffed. "And doing everything possible to show her resistance to renewing our marriage vows, for several weeks now."

Matt squinted. "Why would she do that?"

Sam shrugged. "Isn't it obvious? She has a real problem with commitment."

At least to me.

It couldn't be anything else.

The brothers didn't believe that any more than he wanted to. "Is she abandoning the kids, too?" Dan asked.

Sam frowned. "No, of course not. She loves those little guys."

"Then it's just you that's the problem?" Cullen taunted.

Actually, Sam thought, even more miserably, *I don't know what the problem is.* The two of them clicked. They had always clicked. Until it came time to take their love public in an everlasting way. Then she just started putting up roadblocks even he couldn't get past.

"Is there a point to all this?" Sam asked with a great deal more patience than he felt.

The five men nodded.

"The fact Lulu is trying to call the wedding off,"

Chase said finally, "when it's clear how crazy she is about you, should point you toward some pretty big deficit in your behavior. And if you're smart—" he paused meaningfully, to let his words sink in "—you'll figure out what that is. Pronto."

Friday afternoon, Lulu had just finished taking care of her lone remaining hive when Sam's truck turned into her ranch. Her heart pounding, because she wasn't sure she was quite ready to say all the things she needed to say to him, she drew off her beekeeper's gloves and veil, stepped outside the apiary gate and began moving toward him.

He walked toward her, too, and as he did, she couldn't help but admire how good he looked in the usual jeans, boots, chambray work shirt and stone-colored Resistol slanted across his brow. As he neared, the masculine determination she so admired glinted in his gold-flecked eyes.

Her heart thundered in her chest, as her spirits rose and fell, then rose again.

When she reached him, she stripped off her protective suit and hung it over the porch railing, feeling suddenly achingly vulnerable. "I thought we were going to meet up later," she said with as much feminine cool as she could muster. When she'd had time to clean up and put on something besides an old Texas A&M T-shirt and shorts.

He acknowledged this was so with a dip of his head. "I know what we said before I left to take the kids to preschool."

"But?" Lulu inhaled the brisk masculine fragrance of his aftershave.

"I didn't want to waste any more time."

Funny, she didn't, either. But would they be able to work it out? The way they hadn't before?

In that instant, she decided they would.

Taking her by the hand, he led her up the steps to the front porch. Sat down with her in the wooden rocking chairs she'd inherited from her late grandmother and brought his chair around until they were facing each other, knee to knee.

His eyes were full of the things she'd almost been afraid to hope for, his gaze leveled on hers. "I want to start over, Lulu," he continued, his voice a sexy rumble. His hands tightened protectively on hers. "And this time keep working at it, until we get it right." He looked at her with so much tenderness she could barely breathe.

Her heart somersaulted in her chest. She drew in a shuddery breath. "You mean that?" she whispered.

He nodded soberly and hauled in a rough breath. Shaking his head in regret, confessed, "I never should have pressured you into staying married to me. Like it was some kind of social contract or means to an end. Because you're right, Lulu." He stood and pulled her to her feet. Wrapping his arms around her, he brought her even closer, so they were touching in one long, comforting line. "A real marriage is so much more than that. It's about promising your whole heart and soul."

He paused, all the love and commitment she had ever wanted to see shining in his eyes. "It's about vowing to stay together no matter what for the rest of your lives. And that's what I want with you, Lulu," he confessed. "To be with you for the rest of our lives. Because I love you. I've always loved you. And I always will."

Tears of joy and relief blurred her vision. "Oh, Sam," she said, hugging him tight. "I love you, too."

He paused to kiss her, demonstrating the depth of his feelings in a most effective way.

She kissed him back, sweetly and tenderly, letting him know she felt the same.

When they finally drew apart, Lulu confessed raggedly, "But I've made so many mistakes, too."

His gaze holding hers, he listened.

She swallowed around the lump in her throat and pushed on. "The biggest one was not letting you know that I never fell out of love with you. Not at the time we broke up. Not during all those years when we were apart." Her lips curving ruefully, she shifted even closer. "And certainly not the last couple of months."

His hand slid down her spine, soothing, massaging, giving her the courage to finally convey what was in her heart. "Then why didn't you want to say that in your vows to me?"

She drew a shuddery breath and clutched at him, reveling in his heat and his strength. "I was so happy, just living with you and the triplets. I was afraid to upset the status quo. Afraid if I told you how I really felt, only to find that you didn't still love me the way you once had, that it would change things or put too much pressure on us. Somehow ruin things, the way our elopement did."

He sat down again, pulling her onto his lap. "I take the responsibility for that." Regret tightened the corners of his lips. "I knew you weren't ready to marry me at nineteen."

Looking back reluctantly, she remembered his initial hesitation. Realized, too late, it was a warning she should have heeded. "Then why *did* you say yes, when I suggested eloping with Peter and Theresa?" she asked curiously.

His mouth twisted in a rueful line. "It was selfishness.

I was so damn in love with you, and I was graduating college and about to head back to Laramie. I wanted you with me, even if it wasn't the right thing for you. And deep down, you knew we were too young to make that kind of lifelong commitment, too."

"Otherwise I wouldn't have been so afraid and ashamed to tell everyone we'd gotten hitched."

A contemplative silence fell while they both came to terms with the past.

"Even so..." She put her hands across the warm, solid wall of his chest. "I shouldn't have asked you to hide our marriage. Especially when I know now it made you feel like I was ashamed of my feelings for you. I wasn't. I was just afraid of what people would think...that they'd assume I was being reckless and impulsive again." She sighed. "And most of all? I was afraid of disappointing you and ruining everything between us. And *that* I really couldn't take."

"We both made mistakes." The pain in his low tone matched the anguish she'd felt in her heart. "Years ago. And recently, too." He pressed a kiss to her temple, her brow. "I never should have walked out on you when you told me you didn't want to go through with our recommitment ceremony. I should have given you all the time you needed."

Tingles sliding through her head to toe, Lulu called on the perspective she, too, had gained. "I had enough time to figure out what was in my heart."

His brow lifted.

Feeling the thud of his heart beneath her questing fingertips, she confessed in a tone overflowing with soul-deep affection, "You taught me how to love. How to be vulnerable. And how to risk."

He grinned with the shared realization that they'd finally found the happiness they'd both been craving.

"And that being the case…" She recited her feelings in an impromptu version of the vows he'd been wanting her to pen, "I pledge my past, my present and my future to you. I promise to be your wife and take you as my husband forevermore. And—" she hitched in a bolstering breath, looking deep into his eyes "—I promise to do everything I can to make you happy, Samuel Kirkland. To give love and accept it in return. Because I do love you," she finished thickly, knowing she'd never be able to say it enough, "so very, very much…"

Sam's eyes gleamed. "I love you, too, sweetheart," he murmured, bending her backward from the waist and bestowing on her the kind of jubilant kiss couples engaged in at the end of their nuptials.

Grinning, he brought her upright. "And as long as we're speaking about what's in our hearts… I want to thank you for teaching me what love is and making my life so much happier and brighter than I thought it could ever be. For giving us…and the boys…a future." Voice rusty, he went down on one knee. "So, if you'll have me, Lulu McCabe, I vow to love, cherish and protect you for as long as we both shall live." He reached into his pocket and brought out a diamond engagement ring.

"Oh, I'll have you, Sam Kirkland!" Tenderness streaming through her, Lulu drew him to his feet. She gave him another long kiss. "For the rest of my life!"

"You know," Sam teased, when the steamy caress had ended and the ring was on her finger, "our spur of the moment vows were really spectacular."

And heartfelt, Lulu thought. On both sides. "So much so that I kind of feel married again," she teased. Even without the wedding rings.

"Really married," he agreed. Sobering, he went on, "But I still think we should make our union as strong and official as it can be."

And that meant going public with their commitment.

"I'm with you, cowboy." Lulu beamed, excited to tell him the rest. "Luckily for us, there's still a wedding planned for tomorrow at my parent's ranch."

He grinned his sexy, mischievous smile that she loved so much. "You didn't cancel it?"

Lulu wreathed her arms about his shoulders and gazed up at him adoringly. "I couldn't. Not when I still wanted to spend the rest of my life with you so very much."

He sifted a hand through her hair, then drawled happily, "Sounds like we'd better get a move on then, darlin', as I imagine there's still a lot to do."

"We'll handle it," Lulu told him confidently. "And while we're at it, we'll enjoy every moment, every step of the way. Because this time, my love—" she rose on tiptoe to give him another lengthy reunion kiss "—we're doing it right."

Epilogue

One year later

"Mommy, can we take Beauty to court with us?" Ethan asked.

Lulu wasn't surprised the triplets wanted their beloved pet to accompany them. It was going to be an exciting day.

"No, honey." She knelt to help him clip on the tie he had insisted on wearing, because he wanted to be just like Daddy. Who was looking mighty fine, in a dark suit, pale blue shirt and tie.

Sam assisted Andrew with his neckwear. Theo had figured his tie out on his own and didn't need any assistance.

"How come?" Andrew asked, gently petting the top of Beauty's head.

"Dogs aren't allowed in court," Sam explained. "Unless they're service dogs. Like the ones some of Uncle Matt's friends have."

"That wear the special vests," Ethan said. "And help the old soldiers."

"Ex-soldiers, and yes, that's right." Sam grinned.

The boys thought about that for a minute. "Then could we take some of Mommy's bees with us?" Ethan asked.

Sam shook his head. "They need to stay on the Honeybee Ranch."

"So they can make more honey," Andrew said.

"Right." Lulu smiled.

"How many hives do you have?" asked Theo, who was always counting something.

"About three hundred and ten."

Sam had not only created an auxiliary membership that allowed her and other ranchers who did not specialize in cattle to join the Laramie County Cattleman's Association, he had also convinced her she could do more than one thing. So she'd brought the colony back from Wisconsin, nurtured them through the stress of posttravel and added a few more boxes in the spring.

She'd also hired an assistant beekeeper to stay on the property and do a lot of the day-to-day work for her business, so she could concentrate on caring for Sam and the boys, who altogether were quite the handful. Especially now that the triplets had gone from two-word sentences to nonstop chatter and endless questions.

As they prepared to leave, Beauty followed them to the door.

"Ahhh," Ethan pouted. "She's going to be lonely without us!"

"Are you sure we can't take her?" Andrew asked.

"She was in the wedding!"

"That was outside, on Grandma and Grandpa's ranch, and she had special permission to be there."

"Yes, but she was really good."

She had been. As had the boys. And it had been a glorious day, full of the promise of a lifetime of love ahead.

Sam got out a dog biscuit for each boy to give the Saint Bernard. "She'll be waiting for us when we get back," he said.

"And we're going to have a huge party!" Andrew spread his hands wide.

"Yes, we are," Lulu promised.

All the McCabes were going to be there in court to witness the big day. And all of Sam's sisters, as well.

Outside the courtroom in the marble-floored hallway, Lulu and Sam paused to speak to the boys. "This is very important," Lulu said gently.

"So you all need to be on your best behavior," Sam continued. "Do you understand?"

The boys nodded.

Sam and Lulu escorted them into the courtroom and took a seat at the table. The clerk announced the adoption procedure.

Hearing their names, all three boys jumped up onto the seats of their chairs, unable to contain themselves.

Andrew yelled, "Do we take this Mommy? Yes!"

Ethan shouted, too. "Do we take this Daddy? Yes!"

Theo clapped his hands. "You may kiss!"

The courtroom full of family erupted in a flood of laughter and tears. Sam and Lulu shot to their feet, too. Together, they lovingly contained their three little charges.

"Sorry, Your Honor," Sam said with as much solemnity as he could manage, "they have wedding and adoption formalities mixed up."

"Well." The judge cleared her throat, looking a little teary-eyed, too. "It's understandable. The depth of commitment is the same."

It absolutely was, Lulu thought.

"So, if y'all think we can continue...?"

Sam and Lulu bent and whispered a new set of instructions to the boys. They nodded solemnly, raised their hands and when called upon, said, "Sorry, Your Honors. We're going to be quiet until we're *allowed* to cheer."

And they were.

Afterward, they gathered outside the courtroom in the hallway. Hugs and congratulations were exchanged all around.

Hours later, when their company was gone and the kids were finally asleep in their beds, Sam and Lulu met up on the back deck for a glass of champagne in the starlight.

He clinked glasses with her and smiled victoriously. "We did it."

She linked arms with him, sipped. "We sure did."

They took a moment to ruminate on all they had accomplished in coming together. Sam slanted her a deadpan glance. "Think we'll ever get that honeymoon?" he teased.

"Oh, maybe twenty years from now," Lulu joked.

They both laughed.

"Seriously." She rose up on tiptoe and kissed him, sweetly and tenderly. With a contented sigh, she drew back just enough to be able to see his face. "It feels like we've been on one since we got back together."

Bliss flowed between them.

Sam gave her waist an affectionate squeeze. His gold-flecked eyes sparkling with joy, he mimed writing in the sky. "Hashtag. Best Life Ever."

* * * * *

*Watch for the next book in Cathy Gillen Thacker's
Texas Legends: The McCabes miniseries,
coming December 2019,
only from Harlequin Special Edition!*

Available August 20, 2019

#2713 THE MAVERICK'S WEDDING WAGER
Montana Mavericks: Six Brides for Six Brothers
by Joanna Sims
To escape his father's matchmaking schemes, wealthy rancher Knox Crawford announces a whirlwind wedding to local Genevieve Lawrence. But his very real bride turns out to be more than he bargained for—especially when fake marriage leads to real love!

#2714 HOME TO BLUE STALLION RANCH
Men of the West • by Stella Bagwell
Isabelle Townsend is finally living out her dream of raising horses on the ranch she just purchased in Arizona. But when she clashes with Holt Hollister, the sparks that result could have them both making room in their lives for a new dream.

#2715 THE MARINE'S FAMILY MISSION
Camden Family Secrets • by Victoria Pade
Marine Declan Madison was there for some of the worst—and best—moments of Emmy Tate's life. So when he shows up soon after she's taken custody of her nieces, Emmy isn't sure how to feel. But their attraction can't be ignored... Can Declan get things right this time around?

#2716 A MAN YOU CAN TRUST
Gallant Lake Stories • by Jo McNally
After escaping her abusive ex, Cassie Smith is thankful for a job and a safe place to stay at the Gallant Lake Resort. Nick West makes her nervous with his restless energy, but when he starts teaching her self-defense, Cassie begins to see a future that involves roots and community. But can Nick let go of his own difficult past to give Cassie the freedom she needs?

#2717 THIS TIME FOR KEEPS
Wickham Falls Weddings • by Rochelle Alers
Attorney Nicole Campos hasn't spoken to local mechanic Fletcher Austen since their high school friendship went down in flames over a decade ago. But when her car breaks down during her return to Wickham Falls and Fletcher unexpectedly helps her out with a custody situation in court, they find themselves suddenly wondering if this time is for keeps...

#2718 WHEN YOU LEAST EXPECT IT
The Culhanes of Cedar River • by Helen Lacey
Tess Fuller dreamed of being a mother—but never that one memorable night with her ex-husband would lead to a baby! Despite their shared heartbreak, take-charge rancher Mitch Culhane hasn't ever stopped loving Tess. Now he has the perfect solution: marriage, take two. But unless he can prove he's changed, Tess isn't so sure their love story can have a happily-ever-after...

YOU CAN FIND MORE INFORMATION ON UPCOMING HARLEQUIN® TITLES, FREE EXCERPTS AND MORE AT WWW.HARLEQUIN.COM.

HSECNM0819

*After escaping her abusive ex, Cassie Zetticci is
thankful for a job and a safe place to stay at the
Gallant Lake Resort. Nick West makes her nervous
with his restless energy, but when he starts teaching her
self-defense, Cassie begins to see a future that involves
roots and community. But can Nick let go of his own
difficult past to give Cassie the freedom she needs?*

*Read on for a sneak preview of
A Man You Can Trust,
the first book—and Harlequin Special Edition debut!—
in Jo McNally's new miniseries, Gallant Lake Stories.*

"Why are you armed with pepper spray? Did something
happen to you?"

She didn't look up.

"Yes. Something happened."

"Here?"

She shook her head, her body trembling so badly
she didn't trust her voice. The only sound was Nick's
wheezing breath. He finally cleared his throat.

"Okay. Something happened." His voice was gravelly
from the pepper spray, but it was calmer than it had been
a few minutes ago. "And you wanted to protect yourself.
That's smart. But you need to do it right. I'll teach you."

Her head snapped up. He was doing his best to look at her, even though his left eye was still closed.

"What are you talking about?"

"I'll teach you self-defense, Cassie. The kind that actually works."

"Are you talking karate or something? I thought the pepper spray…"

"It's a tool, but you need more than that. If some guy's amped up on drugs, he'll just be temporarily blinded and really ticked off." He picked up the pepper spray canister from the grass at her side. "This stuff will spray up to ten feet away. You never should have let me get so close before using it."

"I didn't know that."

"Exactly." He grimaced and swore again. "I need to get home and dunk my face in a bowl full of ice water." He stood and reached a hand down to help her up. She hesitated, then took it.

Meg tensed from head to toe, sucking in her breath as she
saw two masculine hands close over the shutters' edges on
either side of her body. Then instinctively turned her head to
take in light hair, a strong stubbled jaw and blue eyes—no
more than an inch from hers.

"I… I…" He smelled good. Not sweaty at all, the way
she surely did. The firm muscles in his arms bracketed her
shoulders.

"I think I got it if you just wanna kinda duck down under
my arm." Despite the awkward situation and the weight of
the shutter, the suggestion came out sounding entirely good-
natured.

And okay, yes, separating their bodies was an excellent
idea. Because she wasn't accustomed to being pressed up
against any other guy besides Zack, for any reason, not even
practical ones. And a stranger to boot. Who on earth was this
guy, and how had he just magically materialized in her yard?

The ducking-under-his-arm part kept her feeling just as
awkward as the rest of the contact until it was accomplished.
And when she finally freed herself, her rescuer calmly,

competently lowered the loose shutter to the ground, leaning it against the house with an easy "There we go."

He wore a snug black T-shirt that showed his well-muscled torso—though she already knew about that part from having felt it against her back. Just below the sleeve she caught sight of a tattoo—some sort of swirling design inked on his left biceps. His sandy hair could have used a trim, and something about him gave off an air of modern-day James Dean.

"Um… I…" Wow. He'd really taken her aback. Normally she could converse with people she didn't know—she did it all summer every year at the inn. But then, this had been no customary meeting. Even now that she stood a few feet away, she still felt the heat of his body cocooning her as it had a moment ago.

That was when he shifted his gaze from the shutter to her face, flashing a disarming grin.

That was when she took in the crystalline quality of his eyes, shining on her like a couple of blue marbles, or maybe it was more the perfect clear blue of faraway seas.

That was when she realized…he was younger than her, notably so. But hotter than the day was long. And so she gave up trying to speak entirely and settled on just letting a quiet sigh echo out, hoping her unbidden reactions to him didn't show.

Need to know what happens next?
Find out when you order your copy of
The One Who Stays *by Toni Blake,*
available August 2019 wherever you buy your books!

www.Harlequin.com

PHTBEXP0819